CREEP CON

★ ★ ★

CREEP CON

★★★

Kim Firmston

James Lorimer & Company Ltd., Publishers
Toronto

James Lorimer & Company Ltd., Publishers acknowledges the support of the Ontario Arts Council. We acknowledge the support of the Canada Council for the Arts which last year invested $24.3 million in writing and publishing throughout Canada. We acknowledge the Government of Ontario through the Ontario Media Development Corporation's Ontario Book Initiative.

Cover design: Tyler Cleroux
Cover image: yves Tennevin, Flickr

Library and Archives Canada Cataloguing in Publication

Firmston, Kim, author
    Creep con / Kim Firmston.

Issued in print and electronic formats.
ISBN 978-1-4594-0998-9 (bound).--ISBN 978-1-4594-0977-4 (pbk).--ISBN 978-1-4594-0978-1 (epub)

    I. Title.

PS8611.I75C74 2015   jC813'.6   C2015-903535-X
                                              C2015-903536-8

James Lorimer &   Canadian edition   American edition
Company Ltd., Publishers   (978-1-4594-0977-4)   (978-1-4594-0998-9)
117 Peter St., Suite 304   distributed by: distributed by:
Toronto, ON, Canada   Formac Lorimer Books   Lerner Publishing Group
M5V 2G9   5502 Atlantic Street   1251 Washington Ave N
www.lorimer.ca   Halifax, NS, Canada   Minneapolis, MN, USA
                              B3H 1G4   55401

Printed and bound in Canada.
Manufactured by Friesens Corporation in Altona, Manitoba, Canada in May 2016.
Job #222756

Dedicated to my daughter, Emily Firmston, who is both an amazing writer and a walking database for all things anime. This book wouldn't have been as good without her constant help.

Dedicated as well to the awesome Otafest organizers and volunteers who remain constantly vigilant and make this annual anime conference safe and fun for everyone.

CONTENTS

★ ★ ★

CHAPTER ONE

THE TELEPORTING CLASSROOM

Fifty sit-ups, ten minutes of shadowboxing, and a twelve-minute jog later, my stress level isn't any lower than when I woke up. Luckily breakfast was only a cup of tea, groceries being a bit scarce until Mom gets paid, so I'm not likely to barf. Still, to say I'm nervous might be the world's biggest understatement. I'm panicked, overwhelmed, terrified. This big-city high school is as huge as the wool-grey sky above it. The fact that this single Calgary high school holds one-third of the students in *all* the Fort McMurray schools is more than enough reason to freak me out. Not to mention I'm late. Not by the clock. I still have fifteen minutes before classes. I'm late in the year. Spring break ended the week before last. I mean, I really don't know how this situation could be any more awkward.

Or horrible.

Small, pricking snowflakes blow in white loops against the students who push past. They pull their hoods tight against the stabbing cold and quick-walk into the building. But I stand here, frozen, my breath coming in small icy puffs.

In my imagination I set this moment in a frame. The

opening panel of a comic book. My normal life right before everything goes haywire. But I guess that would have been a few comic books ago — starting with Rose.

Rose and I had been walking together. A late night of making props for our school's upcoming presentation of *Alice in Wonderland* had kept us out past dark. Still, we each had walked home a million times, so neither of us were worried. Not even when a rattling, beater of a truck slowed down and a kid, probably eighteen years old or so, leaned out the window and yelled to us, "Shake that ass! Come on, bitches!"

We flipped him off. Told him to get lost. We even joked, as he drove away in the direction of Tower Road, about what a frustrated, blue-balled jerk he was. We never thought anything more would happen.

We walked another two blocks chatting about how cool the gigantic tea set was. I thought I heard the truck again, but when I looked around, I didn't see anything. I still remember that buzz of uneasiness that vibrated just under our goodbyes as we parted. I wish I had listened to it. Known what it was. But I turned down my street, excited to tell Mom about my day's adventures. Rose continued on, heading the three blocks to her house.

Except she didn't make it.

It wasn't until the next day when her desk was empty and the rumours were flying that I found out she had been raped a block from home.

It could have been me.

From there we go to the next comic in the series — my mom's friend, Mei, opening a diner in Calgary and offering my mom a job. Mom jumped at the chance to get us out of Fort McMurray, claiming it was so I could get a better education.

To give me more opportunities. To get me into a good university. I played along. Even with Grandma Poitras's help I was still jumping at every rattling truck engine, every playful hoot, every wolf-howl whistle.

And that gets me to here. New city, new school, no friends. Still, it's time to move along in my latest comic from panel one to panel two.

I start walking.

Inside the doors, voices echo off the walls and students clump in groups of two and three. I swing my backpack off one shoulder and pull out the school map. A drip of melting snow falls from my hair onto the orange paper. In my attempt to wipe it away I smudge the ink, eliminating an entire classroom. That's okay. I probably didn't need that one anyway. I try to orient myself, but I'm faced with one staircase and three hallways that aren't where they should be. I turn the map around and pick a direction. Step one — find my locker.

The hallway is packed shoulder to shoulder. Yelled conversations about cute boys and hockey, makeup, and homework fill the space. I'm jostled as I read the locker numbers, getting turned around twice until I have no idea where I am anymore.

I'm studying the increasingly crumpled map when an elbow knocks my arm. The map flies from my fingers, fluttering right into the middle of a group of girls wearing nearly identical knitted sweaters and factory ripped jeans. Their sparkly runners twist as they talk about the hot substitute teacher in chemistry while giggling at a pitch slightly higher than a suffering chipmunk. I debate if, with a quick dart of my arm, I can reach in and snatch my map back unnoticed.

Then, a sparkly sneaker lands on it.

Frustrated heat rises up my neck. I want to spin around and leave. Leave the map, leave the school, leave to be anywhere but here. Except . . . Mom is probably going through the exact same thing right now. Well, maybe not the *exact* same thing but it's day five at her new job and I know she's having a hard time. Work has kept her late nearly every day, we're still living out of boxes, and groceries are starting to run thin. We only just got internet last night. But Mom can't quit. Quitting would have us out on the street. It isn't an option for her.

And it isn't an option for me.

I lift my chin and use my trusted and true technique that always gets me through difficult situations. I imagine the group of girls in a comic book. Looking at them this way, I realize they aren't super-villains, just popular kids. Nothing to be afraid of. I mean, Batgirl could handle this easily. So can I.

I clear my throat and address the girl in ridiculously ripped skinny jeans as her shoe grinds my map into the ground. "Um," I say, my speech a wavering imitation of the bold and heroic voice I'd like to use. "You're standing on my map."

"Huh?" The girl looks down. "Oh, sorry about that!" She snatches it from under her foot and, handing it back, asks, "Are you new?"

I nod, brushing off the muddy shoe mark and smearing away another classroom. "I can't find my locker."

She leans over and has a look. "You're in the wrong hall." She turns the map around in my hand, then points. "Go that way. It will be on your left."

"Thanks," I say, turning away. Maybe these big-city kids aren't so bad.

The girl's directions are good. I find my locker and pull out the combination written on a slip of paper. It takes three tries and some jiggling before the door swings open, letting loose the stench of old Cheetos and ripe sneakers. Making a mental note to bring some air freshener tomorrow, I put my things away, then use my timetable to figure out what I need for my first two classes. So far so good.

Step two — find class. Holding the damp and dirty map the right way up this time, I follow the hallways until I find a set of stairs. My class is on the second floor. I think. There are eight sets of stairs in this school. I'm hoping this is the right one.

On the second floor the crowd has thinned. I look at the room numbers. Again they don't match with the map. Maybe I was wrong. Maybe my class is on the main floor. Or maybe they have a different second floor. This school is so confusing. I see another set of stairs and head back to the main floor and a near empty hall. The bell for class rings. I'm out of time.

I look in the direction of my locker. Or the direction my locker *might* be in, a knot of anxiety pinching my chest. I see myself wandering this labyrinth for the rest of my life — my shoes wearing away, students coming and going, and me becoming *the ghost girl who wanders the hall.* That makes me smile. I mean, I might be late, but being lost that long is just silly. I flip the map around again and start to walk when I'm hit from behind and knocked bodily into the lockers.

"Oh, god! I'm so sorry." A long-limbed girl with black, lambs-wool hair and deep brown eyes stares up at me from the ground. She has a green satchel with a winged symbol on it slung across her chest and a binder full of blank papers open beside her.

I reach out to her. "Are you all right?"

"Yeah. Thanks." She takes my hand and stands up, dusting her knees, and scooping up her binder. "Sorry, rushing . . . somewhere."

"Are you lost?" I ask.

"Yeah, it's my second week in this place and I still can't find all my classrooms on the first try."

I nod. "I'm lost too. I'm trying to find room 111, Social twenty-dash-one but . . ." I shrug.

The girl gives me a huge smile, showing off silver braces. "That's the classroom I'm looking for! Want to be lost together?"

"Sure!" I say. "I'm Mariam."

"Tya," she returns.

I look down the deserted hallway. "I thought the classroom was on the second floor, but I couldn't find it there. Mind you, I can't find it down here either."

"Maybe," Tya whispers, hand held by her mouth, "it teleports."

I laugh and together we continue our hunt. Inside the classrooms I can hear instructions being given. I'm glad Tya's with me. Now I don't have to walk into a full classroom completely alone.

"Just be glad this isn't the campus from *Hyakko*," she says.

"The campus from what?" I ask.

"Oh," her smile falters, "Never mind. Anime reference. Here it is."

"Our two lost students!" the teacher announces, seeing us through the door. "Come on in." He ticks us off the list and we head to the only remaining desks at the front of the room. Tya unslings her satchel from her shoulder, digging inside. I open my blue spiral-bound notebook and search my backpack for my Eleventh Doctor sonic screwdriver pen — a goodbye gift from Kaitlin and Cora. I glance over at Tya as she starts copying the notes off the board with . . . an Eleventh Doctor sonic screwdriver pen.

No way.

★★★ CHAPTER TWO

ONE HUNDRED PERCENT JAMAICAN *OTAKU*

Tya sees my pen and grins full force.

I mouth the words, "Do you like *Doctor Who*?" under the sound of the teacher's squeaking black marker.

"Totally," Tya whispers. "Have you watched *Attack on Titan*?"

I shrug and shake my head. "Have you read *Birds of Prey*?"

She raises an eyebrow like she has no idea what I'm talking about.

At the whiteboard, the teacher clears his throat, his marker silent. "Ladies. Am I interrupting something?"

We both shake our heads and return to furiously jotting notes, sonic screwdrivers racing.

The class continues for the full eighty-eight minutes the school board has determined we need to be educated. Luckily Mr. Perez isn't dead boring. He's actually one of those guys who likes stirring up conflict. Of course this almost leads to a fist fight over immigration and nationalism within the first half hour. Personally, I don't mind immigration, especially since that was how my mom came to Canada from the Philippines. Then again, with a spring storm blowing like a banshee on the

16

window panes, I sometimes question her decision to leave the heat of her homeland.

The bell rings and we grab our things. Tya walks with me into the hall. "So, you like sci-fi stuff, huh?" she asks.

I laugh. "I like *Doctor Who*, but I'm more into comics and superheroes. You?"

"Anime and manga all the way," she says. "*Doctor Who* as of last year. If you like comics you must read the webcomic *Homestuck*. Everyone's into that."

I frown. "Nah, sorry. What kind of anime do you like?"

"*Shoujo*, mostly."

"I don't even know what that is." I laugh.

"Yeah, well," Tya shrugs, her eyes focusing on her runners.

I get the feeling in her old school she probably didn't need to explain what *shoujo* was. Just like how I wouldn't have to explain who the *Birds of Prey* were to Kaitlin and Cora. But maybe . . . "Want to get together at lunch?" I offer. "You can fill me in on this *shoujo* stuff and I can tell you all about my comics."

Tya lets loose a wide, glinting smile. "That would be perfect! What do you have next?"

I look at my schedule on the back of the rather wrecked up map. "Bio. You?"

"Aww, I have art." Tya scrunches her nose. "Meet at the cafeteria after?"

"Sure!" I say. "If I can find it."

Tya laughs. "Good point. Why don't we exchange phone numbers? That way we can talk to each other while we're wandering the hallways."

"Our cell phones dying minute by minute . . ." I add, hand held to my brow in the sign of desperation.

"I can totally picture that!" Tya laughs. She pulls out her cell.

I pull out my notebook. I have an old hand-me-down phone, the kind that, if I were to be kidnapped, I'd be too embarrassed to use. Mom says having an old phone is better than having no phone, but I'm not so sure about that.

Tya and I part at the bottom of the nearest staircase, and wish each other luck. Then I tackle my next quest, finding Bio twenty. This turns out to be not as hard as earlier. My classroom is right by the top of the stairs.

This time eighty-eight minutes seems more like three hours. Mrs. Parsons, the biology teacher, keeps losing control of the class and most of the lesson is spent with her yelling "Pay attention!" Finally the bell rings for lunch. After briefly forgetting I'm on the second floor, I finally get my bearings and head down nearest stairwell, magically ending up by my locker. I stash my books and grab the white plastic grocery bag my lunch is wrapped in.

Suddenly I'm all nerves again. What will Tya think of my homemade lunch? I don't know how kids are around here. Will I be the only one in the whole cafeteria with a lunch from home? Will they think I'm some kind of idiot? I consider throwing my lunch in the garbage or keeping it in my locker. I mean, I can just pretend I forgot my lunch money or say I'm not hungry so no one knows I'm actually too broke to eat cafeteria food. But then again, I *am* hungry, really hungry, especially since I haven't eaten anything yet. Besides, I have the chicken chow mein Mom brought home from the diner last night. It's not nearly as good as the homemade *pancit habhab* Mom usually makes on Sunday night, but I've been looking forward to those noodles all morning.

"Anyway," I scold myself, "there is no way I'm the only one

who brings their own lunch. How could it be a problem?" Still, I hide the lunch bag in my backpack under a couple of comic books. Not the coolest disguise, but good enough.

Tya isn't outside the cafeteria when I get there. I poke my head through the door. It's wild and noisy with a strong smell of grease. Pretty much the same as my old school. Of course Cora, Kaitlin, and I usually holed up in the art room to eat, so this is a little overwhelming. Still, I don't run, even though my brain is begging me to take off, give up, go home. I really want to find my new friend. I want this to work. "Batgirl could do this," I mutter under my breath. "I can do this."

A few steps in and I spot Tya at a corner table. She waves madly with arms crisscrossing mid-air. "Hey, you found me!" Tya says.

"Yeah, the cafeteria tried to teleport but I jumped just in time," I joke, sitting down, hiding my nerves.

In front of her Tya has a small black box with pink blossoms, matching chopstick case, and a thermos with what I think might be a Pokémon on it. She opens her box to reveal raw vegetables cut into flowers, an egg in the shape of a rabbit, and two rice balls with smiling faces. Then, to my surprise, she removes this upper tray revealing sushi in a compartment below.

"Wow!" I stare. "That's some lunch. Did you buy it here?" These city schools are way fancier than anything I've ever seen.

Tya shakes her head. "No. This is my bento. I don't like cafeteria food, so I bring my own."

The sushi looks like it came out of a top-notch restaurant in Tokyo or something. "You made all that?"

"I did."

"Are you part Japanese?"

"No, I'm one hundred percent Jamaican *otaku*," Tya smiles.

"*Otaku*?" I ask.

"Anime fan. You don't watch anime at all, do you?" Tya asks, sounding disappointed.

"Not unless you count *Teen Titans Go!*" I answer, pulling my lunch from inside my backpack and scooping out noodles with chopsticks of my own. Not fancy ones in their own case, but chopsticks all the same. Tya looks impressed.

"I've seen *Teen Titans Go!*" she says. "I would count that as anime. What are you into, then?"

"Right now, the *Birds of Prey*, an all-female crime fighting team who exist just barely inside the law. Here. I'll show you." I pull out my *Birds of Prey* comic and my *Batgirl* one too.

"Wow! These look so cool!" Tya says, flipping through them.

I smile. "You can borrow them if you like. I've read both at least three times already."

"Thanks! So you like female heroes, huh?" Tya asks.

"Pretty much. I got kind of sick of the dark and gloomy sausage-fest most of the other comics had going on. It's just not my world. Besides Batgirl is an amazing superhero. She fights for justice instead of the usual tragedy and revenge thing. She's tough, smart, fun, *and* she knows how to party!"

Tya opens her satchel. "Then, I have some stuff you might like." She pulls out two paperback novel-looking things with writing on the front and the cover on the back. She introduces each one as she hands them to me. "*Ouran High School Host Club* and *Fairy Tail*."

I turn the books over in my hands. "These are called manga, right?" I ask.

Tya grimaces like I just raked my nails over a chalkboard. "You're saying it wrong. It's a Japanese word. The ma is pronounced like when you whine, *Mommmm!*"

"I never whine."

"I'm sure you don't." Tya grins. "The second character is n like in nut, and the last is ga like, well, the noise a baby makes I guess. Ma-n-ga, okay?"

I try saying the word the right way. Tya seems satisfied.

"So how do you read these?" I ask as I encounter the first page with big print screaming, YOU'RE READING IN THE WRONG DIRECTION!

"Oh, yeah, you need to start at the back. Or back for us North Americans anyway. The lines aren't backwards but you read all the panels and word balloons from right to left. Don't worry, it doesn't take long to get the hang of it."

"Okay, sounds good. I would recommend reading my comics in the opposite direction," I say.

"Thanks for the advice," Tya winks.

"So what are these about?" I ask, flipping through *Ouran High School Host Club* and immediately seeing panels with flowers and gorgeous, smiling men.

"*Ouran* is a *shoujo* manga, which just means that it's written for girls, so there's a focus on relationships and storylines. *Fairy Tail* is *shonen*, boys manga, so it has lots of action, but this one also some really great female characters too."

"So *shoujo* is romance?"

"Not always, it covers lots of genres. I mean the lead character in *Ouran High School Host Club* doesn't even realize she's in love until the end of the series."

"So what's it about?"

Tya opens the manga. "A girl named Haruhi," she points at

a short-haired character wearing a baggy sweater, pants, and glasses, "starts at an elite rich kids' high school on a scholarship. She's trying to find a quiet place to study but ends up finding the host club."

"What's a host club?" I ask.

"It's a place where girls pay boys to lavish attention on them."

"That sounds really weird. What kind of teacher would approve of a school club like that?"

"I've asked myself that same question quite a few times," Tya says. "I guess the one in *Ouran* is more of a tea club. The girls have tea and cake and the hosts spend time with them."

"For a fee."

"Well, someone has to pay for the supplies."

"Good point." I nod.

"Anyway, Tamaki, that's him," Tya points to a blond surrounded by roses, "thinks Haruhi is a homosexual boy looking for love and offers her their services."

"Really? Homosexual?" I ask.

"It's not such a big taboo in Japanese entertainment as it is in North American stuff. You have a problem with it?"

I shake my head. "No, I just wouldn't have jumped to the same conclusion if someone wandered into a room."

"Tamaki is really good at jumping to conclusions. Haruhi panics and tries to escape but backs into a six million yen vase, smashing it."

"Crap!"

"I know! And since there's no way she can pay for the damage, she is forced to work off her debt as an errand boy."

"More like an indentured servant." I scowl.

"Exactly. But, it gets better. It turns out that Haruhi is

really good with the ladies who come to the host club," Tya continues.

"Because she is really a girl."

"Yes. So Tamaki decides to make her a host too and gets her a proper uniform, contacts, and a haircut."

"And she agrees to all this?" I ask.

Tya shrugs. "Well, hosts make more money, so she can pay off her debt faster."

"Do the other hosts ever figure out she's a girl?"

"One by one. Tamaki is, of course, the last. He's a little dense."

"So does that ruin everything?"

Tya shakes her head. "No, they agree to keep her secret. They like her and she works well for them."

"That's a pretty good story. It kind of reminds me of Shakespeare."

"Yeah," Tya says. "I guess you're right, especially since it has a poor character fooling rich characters *and* crossdressing. You know, if Shakespeare were alive today, I bet he'd be a manga and anime writer."

I laugh, thinking of the bald bard in his big ruff, scratching out comic panels by candlelight.

Tya says, "I like the parts where the host club boys try to figure out Haruhi's working-class lifestyle. Tamaki calls instant coffee 'commoner's coffee,' and he thinks Haruhi's apartment is so small everyone has to sit like they're in gym class, so they don't take up too much room and embarrass her. Most of the time, she is *so* done with rich people and their stupidity."

"Yeah, I can relate to that."

"The best part is, she's not your typical *'oh save me!'* kind of chick."

"Nice!" I nod. "But isn't a host club kind of a sexist thing?"

Tya shrugs. "I don't know. I don't think so. I mean, what's wrong with girls hiring guys to pay attention to them? Especially when they are really cute guys."

I have another look at the character called Tamaki. "He is kind of cute."

Tya laughs. "Actually the whole thing is really a satire. It totally makes fun of itself. All these guys are the typical characters you find in an average *shoujo* and really, the story is pretty ridiculous. I don't think the writers were actually promoting the values of a host club. But," Tya says, her voice dropping in volume, "you don't have to read it if you don't want to."

I pull the book closer, feeling guilty for upsetting Tya. "No, no. It's fine. Let me check it out."

"Okay!" Tya says, going back to her big smile. "I'll send you the link to the anime too. I actually liked it better than the manga."

Through the rest of lunch we talk more about comics and manga, anime, and cartoons. It turns out we like similar stuff, just in different formats. It's kind of fun learning about the whole anime world and Tya seems really interested to hear about all my favorite superheroes and cartoons. We don't have any more classes together but we do make plans to meet up again tomorrow before school.

Before my next class I check my messages. Mom's called. She has to work late, again. Another waitress quit and there's no one to cover the evening shift. That means I'll be having supper on my own for the fourth day in a row, but I can't complain. We need the money. We're in debt from the move, and with food costs and the ridiculous price of rent, money practically leaks out of the bank account. It's like we'll never get ahead no matter how hard we try.

A sigh shrinks my good mood.

I wish pretending this was a comic book *could* fix my real problems.

CHAPTER THREE

IT'S ALL *KAWAII* *BISHOUJO MECHA*

"So, you've joined the tech-savvy world," Kaitlin says, pushing Cora out of the screen with her enthusiasm.

"Sorry," I say. "It took a while to get everything sorted out. I'm still not completely unpacked."

Now that I finally have internet I can meet up with my best friends from Fort McMurray. We promised each other that we would stay close no matter how far apart we actually were. Cora pushes back against Kaitlin so they both fit in our Skype call, her shiny black hair mixing with Kaitlin's straight blonde.

"How are things?" I ask.

"Pretty good," Cora says.

"Any word on Rose?" I ask. "Is she back at school?"

"No." Cora bows her head. "Her phone number has changed and all her accounts are gone. The house is even up for sale."

None of us say anything, though we all feel the same.

"They still haven't caught that guy either," Kaitlin says.

Anger boils up inside me, making my fists clench. "But I gave them a good description. He's got to be local! You guys should track him down. I bet you'd find his truck on Tower Road."

"What do you want us to do, go vigilante?" Cora asks.

"There's no proof the guy who shouted at you was the rapist," Kaitlin says. "Or at least that's what Constable Chan said."

"Besides, we're not superheroes." Cora shrugs.

"Well, you have to do something!" I growl.

Cora's eyes flash the same spirited expression as her social-activist, Chipewyan grandma — Grandma Poitras. "We *are* doing something. We're changing society around here so this kind of thing doesn't happen again."

"Yeah," Kaitlin says. "Grandma Poitras met with the school board to get a self-defense class started for everyone, not just us."

"And she wants to do an anti-rape program for both the girls and the boys," Cora adds.

"We're going to be helping her out with that," Kaitlin says.

"I still wish I could find that guy," I mutter.

"And what?" Cora asks. "Beat the crap out of him?"

"Yeah," I admit. "Then turn him over to the police. Honest." I give a weak smile.

Cora facepalms. "I think you better lay off the Batgirl comics."

Kaitlin clears her throat. "Anyway . . . how are things in Calgary? Meet any cute cowboys?"

"No," I laugh. "No cowboys. The boys are about the same as Fort Mac."

"How's your mom?" Cora asks.

"I wouldn't know. I hardly ever see her anymore." I try to keep the bitter tone out of my voice, but I hear it creeping in anyway.

"With a big move and a new job, it's bound to happen. I remember it was like that when I moved from St. John's.

Same thing," Kaitlin says, trying to be reassuring. "Make any friends?"

"Yeah. One. Her name is Tya. She's new to the school too and super nice."

"What's she like?" Cora asks.

"A total nerd," I tell them. "She's into *Doctor Who* and stuff."

"Great!" Kaitlin gushes, "So what universe does she follow? Marvel, DC, Dark Horse, Image, Titan? Is she into Batman, Superman, Badger, Flash, Justice League, Tank Girl?" Kaitlin frowns. "Or is she one of those dweebs who likes Archie comics?"

"Whoa, slow down there," Cora growls, shoving Kaitlin. "But, yeah, what's she into?"

"Anime, actually," I reply.

"Ohh. One of those," Kaitlin says, her blue eyes narrowing.

"What do you mean?" I ask.

"Yeah, what *do* you mean?" Cora repeats, her scowl deepening.

Kaitlin shrugs off Cora's outrage with an easy grin, "Come on! They don't even speak English. It's all *kawaii bishoujo mecha* with massive eyes, and jiggling boobs." She holds her fingers in peace signs by her head and squints her eyes.

"Yeah," Cora says dryly, "because Power Girl is nothing like that. She keeps her breasts well hidden with that big ol' boob window."

I laugh. "Kaitlin, cartoons and comic books aren't all that different from anime and manga."

"Well," Kaitlin says, starting to pout — a move that always works on her parents, "Superman never cross-dresses."

"But Captain America did," I reply.

"A couple of times," Cora finishes. "Besides. Some anime is pretty cool. I've just finished watching *Samurai Champloo*."

"Shampoo?" Kaitlin scoffs. "What do they do every episode? Dress up in kimonos and wash each other's hair?"

"Champloo not shampoo!" Cora gives Kaitlin a playful smack on the head. Playful, but not gentle.

"Ow!" Kaitlin howls.

"What kind of stuff does Tya watch?" Cora asks, blatantly ignoring Kaitlin's full on sulking.

"Stuff like *Ouran High School Host Club*. I've just started reading it. It's pretty good. Strange, but good. I mean, flower petals come out of nowhere and yeah, there's cross-dressing, but it's really funny and the writing is solid. Besides, Haruhi is just as good as any of our comic book girls. She's really independent and has this whole secret identity thing going on. You might like her."

"Oh no!" Cora laughs. "You're going to turn into a *shoujo* freak for sure."

"See what I mean?" Kaitlin says, "Not English."

Cora and I shake our heads. I ask if they have read the latest Batgirl or Black Canary comic. I'm too broke to stick my head in a comic book store and only part of the online edition is available unless you pay for a subscription. So without insider info, I'm out of luck.

Cora catches me up on the latest adventures, talking about *Teen Titans* and the Bat family too. I might like the girl heroes but Cora is definitely more into the boys — and shirtless scenes.

Kaitlin, who until this time has been slowly coming out of her sulk, starts flapping her hands and gawping like a goldfish.

"What?" Cora and I both ask.

"Oh my god!" she yells. "Mariam, you live in Calgary!"

"Yeah. That's why we're Skyping. You've only figured this out now?" I say.

"No. I mean, you — live — in — Calgary!" Kaitlin squeals, emphasizing words but not making herself any clearer.

"And again I say, duh!"

"What are you getting at, woman?" Cora says, raising her hand to smack Kaitlin one more time.

"Calgary Comic and Entertainment Expo?"

"Oh my god!" we all start shrieking.

"Only the biggest comic con in all of Alberta. You have to go!" Kaitlin demands.

"Except I'm broke," I say.

"Get a job at the diner. Beg your mom. Sell your stuff. You have to. You need to tell us what it's like," Kaitlin insists.

"Mom won't let me go alone."

Kaitlin waves her hand, brushing away my comment. "Then take that Tya girl. She needs to know more about real cartoons."

"Enough!" Cora says, actually smacking Kaitlin again.

"Ow!" Kaitlin yells. "But you gotta go."

CHAPTER FOUR

CAN YOU DEAL WITH DEMONS?

"But, Mommm," I whine. "You guys are always short at the diner. Come on, we need the money and I can do it."

"No!" Her voice is like a whip.

"But why?" I ask, spreading my arms.

"You're too young."

Mom opens the container of stir-fried veggies and sweet and sour pork she brought home from work. She puts a third of it away for my lunch tomorrow, then serves the rest on two plates.

"I'm almost seventeen," I say.

"You have school." Mom collapses into a chair at the kitchen table, a scuffed and stained thing I covered with a red piece of cloth to make it appear nicer. Mom doesn't like things to look too scuzzy, even when they actually are. She starts eating, not looking at me.

I sit down too, my hunger not as sharp as it once was. "I can work after school and on the weekends."

"I didn't move all the way to Canada to have my daughter miss out on her education in order to work."

"I won't miss out."

"What about homework?" Mom asks.

"I can do it between customers, or during study period, or on the bus. Mom, I can work."

"No."

"But why?" I ask.

She looks me in the eye, hard and unmoving. "There are too many creeps."

"I can deal with creeps," I say. "Grandma Poitras taught me —"

"I don't *want* you dealing with creeps," Mom interrupts. "You study. Get good grades. Get lots of scholarships. Go to university. That's your job. My job is to keep you fed, clothed, and housed."

"But I want to help," I pout.

"Not at the diner you don't." The wrinkles by her eyes are deeper. Her smile, which used to be so quick, seems like it has faded away forever.

"Well, what about another job? I could work at the library or at a comic book shop or something. Mom, please."

I take her hand in mine. I know she's only trying to do what's best. But I want her to realize I can take responsibility and help just as much as she does.

She pats my hand, sandwiching it between hers. "It won't be like this forever. Once the diner takes off, they'll be able to pay me more. It's just because it's a new business that things are slow right now."

"I get it, but if you let me get a part-time job, we wouldn't struggle so much."

"There's lots of time for you to act all grown up later."

I frown. "I'm not trying to *act* grown up. I am grown up. Besides, I miss you."

"I'm right here."

"Not all the time. If I worked at the diner we'd see more of each other."

"So you want to be grown up but you still want your mother around." She winks.

I huff in frustration. "Seriously. Mom, there are lots of kids with jobs."

"So let them have the jobs. We'll be fine."

"The fridge is empty."

"Only because I haven't had the time to go grocery shopping. Besides I brought you supper."

"I could go grocery shopping."

"This isn't like Fort McMurray. Calgary is a big city. It's not safe."

I cross my arms. "I told you I'm fine."

"Well, I don't like the thought of you going out on your own. School and home is enough."

"Enough for who?"

Mom rubs her temples. "Just do what I ask until we get settled."

"When will that be?"

Mom ignores me and gets up to put on the kettle.

"Mom?"

"Why do you need to go out? You don't know anyone."

"I made a friend at school. You would know that if you were home once in a while."

"Boy or girl?" Mom asks. "Because if it's a boy then . . ." Mom sputters her irritation. "Well, it just better not be a boy."

"I'm nearly seventeen," I remind her again.

"All the more reason to stay away from them."

"God, Mom! I'm not a child!"

"Don't start yelling!" Mom yells back. "Fine, you have a friend."

"A girl named Tya."

"Good. You can go out with her. No boys."

"At all? Ever?" I ask.

"Not on your own."

"But if she's there, it's okay?"

Mom thumps the counter. "What has gotten into you? You were fine until we came here and now you want to go wandering around the city getting jobs and chasing boys."

"That's not what I said! At all! All I asked was if I could work at the diner! You're blowing this out of proportion!" I take a deep breath and try again. "Okay, we're doing fine for the basics. Rent, food, internet. But what about the rest? Right now, I'd be lucky to get my hands on a second-hand comic. I have no idea what I'd do if any kind of school field trip came up. And the Calgary Comic and Entertainment Expo is right in my backyard now. That's something I could actually go to."

"Those are luxuries."

"Luxuries are important too. Come on. If I worked we could afford more."

"No," Mom says.

"But, why?"

She lays a hand on my shoulder, giving it a squeeze. "Because you're my little girl and it's my job to keep you safe."

"I'm not so little anymore."

"Enough." She ruffles my hair. "Let's not ruin tonight with a big fight. Besides, I'm too tired."

An echo of guilt pangs through me. I hate fighting. It's something I never thought I'd end up doing with my mom.

Never. We've always been close. Then again, I've never asked to get a job before, other than babysitting, or really brought up dating. It's new territory for us in a new city. I guess we're both a little weirded out. I get up and give her a hug. "I'm sorry, Mom. Thanks for working so hard. Please, just think about it."

"Okay," she nods. "Now listen, I have Saturday off. We'll finally have time to unpack the last of those boxes and we can go grocery shopping together too. Then you'll have my undivided attention to tell me all about Super this and Bat that."

"Mom, I'm not that bad!" I laugh. "Though Cora was telling me about the latest Batgirl comic."

"See!" Mom chuckles as her cell phone rings. She rifles through her purse to answer it. "Oh, no," she says to the person on the other line. "Not again." Her face takes on a look of exasperation. "That's the third one! Hang on." Mom looks at me, her eyes steel. "Do you really want a job?"

"Yeah!" I nod.

"Can you deal with demons?"

"If it means I get paid, I can deal with anything."

CHAPTER FIVE

WORLD'S GREATEST BABYSITTER

The demons my mom set me up with greet me at the door, fists pumping in my direction. "Die villain! DIE!" they scream.

"I'm so sorry!" their mom says, pulling them aside and telling them something in quick Korean. "They have a lot of energy."

"It's okay, Mrs. Bin," I say with a smile. "I've got this."

"Great." She searches her purse, pulls out her keys, and gives another distracted glance over her shoulder. "I'll be back at eleven. The kids go to bed at eight. The diner's phone number is on the fridge. If you need anything ask the boys. They can tell you." She yells towards the hallway where the boys have disappeared. "Jim! Sam! Be good!"

Their grinning faces peek around a doorframe. "We will," they chorus.

I know that look. They are planning to be anything but good. Luckily I have a plan or two as well. I lock the door behind their mom and head into the living room, opening my bag as I go. The first thing I pull out are my two massive Hulk fists. They make noise and everything. Mom got them for me a few Christmases ago as a joke. I secretly loved them. Now, their power will be put to good use.

"DOUBLE ATTACK!" the kids yell behind me.

"HULK SMASH!" I scream, spinning around. The Hulk fists let out a *crash*.

The boys stop dead in their tracks. "Cool!" they say in unison. "Can we try?"

"Sure." I smile. I point at the younger brother. "Which one are you, Jim or Sam?"

"I'm Jim!" the older boy states, fists on his hips. "He's Sam!" Then he whispers like he's telling me a big secret. "They're not our real names, though. We really have Korean ones."

"I get it. Secret identities." I nod. "I won't tell anyone."

Jim beams.

"Okay," I say, "Sam, you can try the fists."

"Aww, but what about me?" Jim whines.

"You," I say, digging in my bag again, "can wear this." I pull out my Iron Man mask with voice modulator.

Jim falls to his knees. "You are the most amazing girl I've ever met."

"I know," I say, like it's no big deal. Though really, I'm glad this worked. If these guys were into sports, I'd be at a total loss.

Sam pulls on the Incredible Hulk gloves, smashing them together and producing a sound of destruction. Jim puts on the Iron Man mask. He asks in a robotized voice, "Aren't you afraid we're going to break your stuff?"

"If you break them, they won't be as cool, right?"

The boys nod.

"So, are you going to break them?" I ask.

"No way!" They run off to wage war on each other and the imaginary aliens who have invaded the New York City of their bedroom.

Lucky for them, I've actually grown out of these superhero props. I'm getting more into people I can look up to. Girls who choose their own path and fight for justice in a world where women are treated more like props than people. I mean, Batman and Iron Man are fine, but they don't have my kind of issues. Though I wish I had theirs — I could do so much with a mansion and a bazillion dollars.

But really I like reading about heroes like Batgirl because I can relate. They might have a tragic back story but they don't let it rule their lives. I mean Batgirl broke her spine, but she came back from it, moved into her own place away from Gotham and Batman, and escaped his whole over-domineering parental thing. She's tough and capable, even if she is still young. She doesn't need people to look after her or give her a bunch of rules. She can manage on her own — even if that means having a job, going to school, and fighting crime. She even dates.

Okay, maybe I'm a bit jealous. Still, one day I see myself where she is.

By the time we hit bedtime I've helped the kids build a fort, taken them on a walk where I pretended to see villains on every corner, put them through my superhero training workout with a little of Grandma Poitras's self defense thrown in. I also introduced them to the old Batman show online. It's amazing how much sticking power those campy characters have. Finally I told them bedtime stories, which was really just me reminiscing about my favorite comic books.

Tucking both boys into bed, their eyes barely able to stay open, the older one asks, "Will you come back and play with us again?"

"Why wouldn't I?" I reply.

"Most of our babysitters run away," Sam explains. "Mom says we're mean."

"You aren't mean. You just like to play."

Jim frowns. "I thought girls couldn't like superheroes," he says.

"Who told you that?" I ask.

He shrugs. "I don't know. I just thought they were only for boys."

"Superheroes are for everyone," I say, pulling the covers up to his chin. "And anyone can be a superhero."

"How?" he asks

"Be kind to people. Make them feel happy," I tell him. "Listen to your mom and your teachers. Get good grades in school, so you can be smart like Batman." I try to put in all the stuff that might help his mother out. With these two, she probably needs it.

"We can do that!" the boys yell, jumping out of bed and throwing out their best superhero punches.

It takes another half hour of wrangling the boys back into bed before I'm at the kitchen table, tackling my homework. My cell phone rings with the *Teen Titans Go!* theme song. "Hi," I say.

"How are the demons?" Mom asks.

"Safe and sound. They're really awesome kids."

"You're kidding."

"No. I like them. They're fun," I say.

"You're weird. You know that right?"

Mom and I laugh.

"So what's up?" I ask.

"I have some bad news," she says, sounding really disappointed.

I bite my lip, my heart burning in my chest. She's lost her job. The diner hasn't made it. The doors are closing. We're one paycheque away from ending up homeless. And now we're going to be on the streets.

She continues, "I looked up that Comic Expo thing you were talking about. I was going to surprise you with some tickets."

I breathe a sigh of relief. We're still okay. Then I realize what she's said. "Really?" I beam. "That would be amazing!"

"It's too expensive. We can't afford it. Besides. All that's left is Thursday night. I doubt it's really worth going just for one evening."

In my heart of hearts, I know even Thursday night would be incredible but I don't say that. Instead I reply, "That's fine, Mom. I think I'll be doing a lot of babysitting anyway, so I'll probably be too busy to go. Thanks for thinking of it though, you didn't have to. I'm still looking forward to Saturday. I was thinking maybe we could —"

"Actually," Mom sighs, "I have more bad news. I have to work that day now."

"Oh." I'm actually surprised at how disappointed I feel. Even more so than finding out I can't go to the Comic Expo. "Do you want me to go grocery shopping for you?" I offer.

"No. I'll grab a few things after work. Safeway is right by the diner. I hope that's okay."

I slump in my chair, stare blankly at my homework, and mutter, "It's fine. I'll get the house unpacked while you're at work."

"Thanks Mariam. You're always so understanding."

Yeah, that's what I want to be known for, my awesome ability to be understanding.

CHAPTER SIX

HELPFUL ADVICE

"Comic Expo is out," I tell Cora and Kaitlin Wednesday after school.

"I told you. Get a job," Kaitlin says.

"I did get a job. Babysitting," I return.

"Babysitting pays crap." Cora scowls. "You need a real job."

"I know. But Mom won't let me."

"Get one anyway. Tim Hortons is always hiring."

"Yeah, that would work so well. I can hear the screaming already. It doesn't matter anyway, Comic Expo is practically sold out."

"If you had a real job you could pay a scalper," Kaitlin says. "Then you could tell us all about it."

"Okay, let me lay it out for you," I say, feeling my pulse increase with every point. "Mom won't let me get any job other than babysitting. She won't let me go anywhere alone. She won't let me EVER be near a boy because somehow just being in the vicinity of a male by myself is likely to get me pregnant. And let's not even tackle the subject of dating." I heave a sigh. "I'm totally moving out once I get to university."

"And how are you going to afford that?" Cora asks. "You

would need a decent job so you could put away some money first."

"Arrrgggh! My mom is so frustrating!" I scream.

"Have you talked to her?" Kaitlin asks.

"Yeah. I've also talked to the wall. It's been super-effective," I grumble.

"Well, what about Tya? Is she allowed to go places?" Cora asks, a wicked glint dancing through her dark eyes.

"Yeah, she says her mom pretty much lets her do what she wants."

"So go places with her." Cora says with a shrug.

"Like where?"

Kaitlin shakes her head. "We went through this already. You — are — in — Calgary. You have comic book stores, malls, movie theatres. Go, explore. Live a little."

I grin. It's a solid plan. "I'll talk to Tya. I bet she would really like hitting up a comic book shop." Then another thought strikes me. "Except . . ."

"What now?" Cora asks.

My shoulders slump. "I'm still broke. The lady I'm working for can't pay me until the end of the month."

Kaitlin frowns. "Do Calgary comic book shops have an entrance fee?"

I shake my head. "No, I don't think so."

"So just go look. You're allowed to do that," Kaitlin says.

"Yeah, and bring us back a report. We want the complete rundown. Take some pictures. Be a tourist," Cora orders.

"Okay, okay!" I laugh, excitement bubbling up inside me. "I can do a bit of research, and when I do have money, I'll know where to go."

"I'm looking forward to hearing all about it," Cora says.

"Don't worry, your mom will let up eventually."

"I doubt it," I say. "She seems to think everyone in Calgary is out to get me."

Kaitlin laughs. "That's exactly how people are when they first come to Fort McMurray. Remember? They think it's a big bad boom town full of nasty oil workers. Then they find out it's just a bunch of families and their kids. Everyone is so jumpy when they're in a new place."

"Just give your mom time and keep your activities to yourself. She'll calm down in a month or two." Cora gives me a thumbs-up.

Kaitlin starts bouncing. "Then maybe you can get a real job in the summer," she says. "And when the Comic Expo happens next year you'll have the money to get a ticket."

"Count on it!" I smile. "Thanks, guys. You're the best pep talkers ever."

"Yeah, we're the peppiest," Cora deadpans.

"Oh, I almost forgot to tell you," Kaitlin says. "They finally caught the rapist last night."

"Really?" A shiver shoots through my skin. "How?"

"They say he tried to grab Constable Chan when she was off duty. You know how young she looks."

"She does look young. Is she all right?" I ask.

"It's Constable Chan," Cora scoffs. "She's fine."

I shake my head. "I'm just glad he's off the streets. I was worried about you guys."

Cora flexes one of her biceps. "We're good. You're the single girl in the big city."

I laugh. "I'm good too. It's not as dangerous as you or my mom would think. Besides, thanks to your grandma, I can protect myself."

★★★ CHAPTER SEVEN

RED ROBIN

"And here we are!" Tya announces spreading her arms. "Welcome to Another Dimension! I would say it's my favourite comic shop, but I buy all my manga online so, I don't know too much about this place. Is this all right? Because there are a couple other comic book shops we can hit up if it's not."

My gaze flows over the giant Hulk in the middle of the floor, the rows and rows of comics, the toys, the shirts, the graphic novels. I close my eyes and breathe in the scent of ink and paper, listen to the superhero movie playing on the TV suspended from the ceiling. "Everything is perfect," I sigh.

As soon as I opened glass door the shard of homesickness that had been pressing on my heart melted away. Back in Fort McMurray I had Nerdvana, the local comic book shop, and my second home. Now I feel like everything is finally good again. "I love it."

"Um, okay," Tya says, slowly backing away and bumping into a spinning rack of calendars, knocking one down. "Oh wow, Ultraman!" she says, retrieving it.

"Yeah, they have manga and anime stuff in these places, too," I say.

Tya clicks her heels together and gives me a salute. "Okay, Mariam, give me the tour."

I start walking down the first aisle. Most comic book shops are set up pretty much the same so it's not too hard to get my bearings. "This is the Marvel section," I say.

"Like Avengers," Tya nods.

"Yeah, here." I point to an *Avengers* comic, which is right next to an *Avengers vs. X-Men* comic, which is right next to a *Secret Avengers* comic.

"How do you know which one to read?" Tya asks, looking bewildered.

"They're just different storylines. Pick one that interests you," I say.

"Where's Batgirl?" Tya asks.

"She's not Marvel. We need to find the DC section for her."

We wander around for a bit, Tya as distracted I am by the different things we find along the way, like Batgirl t-shirts, Shakespearean graphic novels, and a variety of *Doctor Who* sonic screwdrivers.

"I know what I'm asking for this birthday," Tya announces.

Finally we arrive in the DC section.

"Woah! Who is this?" Tya asks, picking up a comic.

"Power Girl. She's Superman's cousin from another dimension called Earth 2. She's basically their Supergirl."

"That's quite the costume. Is there a reason for the hole right where her boobs are?"

"Distraction?" I say.

"I'm distracted," Tya laughs.

"I kind of wish they wouldn't draw girls that way."

"Why's that? She has a nice body."

"I guess, but it would be nice if the girls and their costumes looked a little more realistic," I shrug.

"What? Like the guys are so realistic?" Tya says, pointing at a *Justice League* comic. "No one has a six-pack like that."

"But at least they're dressed. I get so sick of the battle bikini. If they could put girls in pasties and a G-string and get away with it, I think they would."

"Yeah, anime is like that sometimes. Have you seen *Kill La Kill*?"

"But it's not realistic," I continue. "The guys get armour and boots. The girls get swimsuits and high heels. It's like, even in battle, girls need to be eye candy. Like it's our only job."

"But aren't comics mostly written for guys?" Tya asks.

"Yeah, but there are lots of girls who like comics too. *I* like comics. And besides even if they are written for guys, shouldn't guys have reasonable expectations?"

"Like girls have reasonable expectations?" Tya says, pointing once again to the unrealistic Justice League six-packs. "I think you're reading too much into this. I'm going to find the manga."

I run my eyes over the comics, looking at all the images. There aren't many of them that represent who I want to be. I hate the low-cut tops, bare arms, and giant shiny breasts. Even Black Canary, who I've always looked up to, ends up in outfits bordering on pornographic more often than not. And it's not just DC comics. Marvel's Black Widow, a butt-kicking, no nonsense spy, is fully dressed, except her zipper is always down to show off maximum cleavage. Like opening up a bullet proof suit to expose your chest is the best thing to do in battle.

At least the newest concept of Batgirl is realistic. Her boobs are reasonable, her outfit is a leather jacket zipped all the way up, and she looks like she could actually do stuff without twisting an ankle or posing with her butt in the air. I pick up the *Batgirl* comic, flipping through the pages, careful not to look like I'm trying to read the whole thing in the aisle, even though I want to.

"So you like Batgirl, do you?" The guy from behind the counter comes up beside me.

I quickly put the comic back on the shelf, my face going red. The guy seems to be about my age. His dark hair is slightly messy. His body looks agile and strong but not overly buff. He has caramel skin and deep brown eyes, sparkling behind his gold-rimmed glasses.

"Uh, yeah, I do," I say, stumbling over my words. "But I wasn't reading it, promise."

"Why not?" he laughs. "I do. Then again, I work here." He smiles. "I'm Samir."

"Mariam," I say, noticing the subtle scent of sandalwood coming off him. "I really wasn't, though. I don't do stuff like that."

"It's fine." He waves his hands, like he's shooing away a fly. "I overheard what you were saying to your friend, about girls not being treated fairly in comics."

"Oh," I say, my face beating hotly in time with my heart. "Yeah. I uh . . ." I look intently at the comics on the shelf. "It's just that . . ."

"I agree with you. I have trouble finding stuff I can give to my niece. She's too old for the little kids' stuff but I don't feel right giving her most of these comics. It's not the kind of thing she should see."

"So why do the artists draw women that way?" I ask, my embarrassment giving way to curiosity. I point to a picture of Starfire in more skin than costume, her huge boobs barely covered. "Is this really how guys think we should be?"

"I guess. Some guys. It does set a pretty bad precedent." He looks back at me and blushes, flapping his hands. "Not me, though. I don't think girls should look like that. Unless they want to. I mean . . . girls can do what they want." He puts his head in his hands. "Uggh."

I laugh. "It's fine. I get it."

He peeks at me, his long black lashes blinking slowly. "Thanks."

"Um, excuse me?" Tya asks, peeking around the aisle. "Do you have the latest *Otomen*?"

Samir turns, pulling his body upright. "Yes, I think it came in this morning. I'll have a look. Give me a second." He rushes into the back.

"Oooh, girl!" Tya whoops, then whispers behind her hand. "He's cute. I think he likes you."

I blush all the more. "He was just being nice, that's all."

"I don't know. You should ask for his phone number or something."

I pick up the *Batgirl* comic once more, studying it with all my concentration. "Um, no."

"Want me to?" Tya offers.

"No." My hands tremble. "I'm fine."

"He works here, so we can come in again." Tya says. "We could come in here lots."

"He probably has a girlfriend and I'm not allowed to date," I say.

Samir comes back with a manga in hand. "Here you go." He hands it to Tya. Then he gives me a copy of *A-Force* — the brand new all-female Avengers team. "Have you read it?"

I shake my head. "I'm more of a DC fan."

"Me too. Red Robin all the way!" He pumps his fist. "Sorry, I like the sidekicks. Batgirl is one of my faves too. But you might enjoy this."

I nod and think of the change left in my pocket. I try to work out if I have enough bus money to pay for the comic. If I don't, I'll have to admit that I came in here with no intention of buying anything. That I'm flat broke and wasting his time. Of course if I use my bus money, it will be a really long walk home. Neither option is great. I shake my head and push the comic back at him, embarrassed beyond belief. "Thanks. But, I can't . . ."

"Oh, you don't need to buy this one. It's mine. I just finished it." He smiles, the corners of his eyes scrunching up. "I just want to know what you think. Read it and then come back and tell me. I'd love to hear your opinion. I work Wednesday to Friday and on Sunday, if you want to stop by." His eyes dip to his toes and he shuffles his feet.

"Uh, thanks." I smile.

Tya's phone rings with the *Pokémon* theme song just as another customer heads to the counter needing Samir's attention and helping to break up the general awkwardness. I return the *Batgirl* comic to the shelf. I'll be back for it at the end of the month. I'll also be back to talk to Samir about *A-Force* — or anything else he wants to discuss.

★★★ CHAPTER EIGHT

I DON'T MIND STICKING OUT

We sit on Tya's bed, propped up by anime body pillows. It's Monday night and technically we're supposed to be doing homework, but in reality Tya is scrolling through her newsfeed.

"Hey, Matt Smith, the Eleventh Doctor, is going to be here for the Calgary Comic and Entertainment Expo."

"Sweet! Do you have tickets?" I ask, suddenly jealous.

Tya shakes her head. "Nah, all my money goes into Otafest."

"What's Otafest?"

"It's an anime festival in May. It's really fun. You should come with me. They have panels, and games, guest speakers, and video rooms, plus tons of other things. It's a big party."

"Sounds amazing, but I don't know if I can afford it right now." I shrug, looking at my lap.

"Oh, don't worry." Tya grins. "I can get the tickets and you can pay me back whenever."

"Is it expensive?" I ask, getting worried.

Tya shakes her head. "Nah, it's a lot cheaper than the Comic Expo, but bring extra money for shopping. Last year I got some really sweet cosplay stuff."

"Okay," I say tentatively. Now that I have a job, I should be able to afford it. So long as Tya isn't picky about waiting for the money. "I'll go."

Tya grabs my hands and starts to bounce. "We can work on our cosplay costumes together!"

"What costumes?" I ask. "Why do I have to dress up as anything?"

"It's more fun that way. Besides," Tya winks, "everyone does it. You'll stick out if you're not dressed up."

"I don't mind sticking out," I shrug.

"Come on!" Tya whines. "Please?"

"What are you going to cosplay as?" I ask, trying to distract her.

"Oh, I don't know. I'm definitely going to do my Erza Scarlet costume from *Fairy Tail*. I love how tough she is. No one messes with Erza."

"Yeah, I remember that from the manga. She's pretty respected."

"If you mean feared, then yeah. Look, here's a picture of me in the costume from two years ago." Tya pulls up a photo onto her laptop. She's essentially wearing a white bandage across her breasts and a pair of flame-decorated martial arts pants cut to calf length. A red wig covers her hair as she poses in a fighting stance.

"Wow! You look killer!" I remark. "I don't know if I could ever show that much skin."

"Oh, that costume isn't too bad. I've seen way worse. Still I don't want to do a repeat costume all weekend. I need at least one new cosplay to show off. Something spectacular. Something that will wow everyone." Tya clicks on Google Images and types in some search words. Pictures of an Asian woman with gold bracelets on her wrists, ankles, and thighs pop up.

"Who's that?" I ask.

"Tharja from the *Fire Emblem Awakening* game."

Tya is completely addicted to *Fire Emblem*. She says she loves the battle strategy but I'm pretty sure it's the romantic setups that have her hooked. She's always talking about her next in-game husband and what couples look cute together.

"Why her?" I ask.

"Tharja's dangerous!" Tya pumps her fist. "She's a dark, spooky, black magic girl who can zap you five ways to hell and back again." Tya enlarges a picture so I can see the costume details. There aren't many. She basically has a loin-cloth, a cape, a barely-there breast holder, and not much else that isn't see-through.

"I couldn't even imagine wearing that in public," I say, hands held over my mouth.

"Don't be so dramatic." Tya types in some new search words then scrolls down through the results. "How about Winry Rockbell from *Fullmetal Alchemist*?"

I consider the picture. I've only seen the first few episodes of this anime and already Winry has won me over. She's the best automail mechanic in the land and turns the whole help-less female thing on its head. Only one problem, she's wearing about as much as Erza.

Tya studies the picture. "It's kind of easy though. Pulling this off wouldn't impress anyone. Unless . . ."

"What?"

Tya throws me an impish grin. "Do you want to go as Edward? You're flat-chested enough to be a boy."

"I'm not going as a boy!" I protest.

"Why not? You get a freaking automail arm!"

"I don't want to cross-dress!"

Tya scowls. "What do you have against cross-dressing?"

"I don't know. I don't mind if others do it. I really don't. And I don't mind reading about it in manga either. But . . . I guess I'm just not used to it as a real-life thing. It's not like I see a lot of it regularly."

"Are you sure? I know Western entertainment is different from Japanese stuff, but there is cross-dressing in our stuff too. Guys dress as girls for comedy. Girls pretend to be guys to get a leg up in society. Look at Mulan. She's a freaking Disney princess."

"I guess."

Tya points to the picture of Edward Elric. "If you dressed as him it wouldn't mean you suddenly turned into a boy or even that you liked girls. It's just a character. Gender isn't such a be all and end all. I don't know why you're so stuck on this."

"I guess you're right," I say eventually. "I mean, don't get me wrong, I just never really thought of dressing as a boy before."

"So you'll do it?" Tya asks, brightening.

"No," I say, giving her a playful shove. "Because I'm still not *that* flat-chested."

"Touchy, touchy," Tya giggles. "Fine, I'll keep looking." She scrolls some more. "Ohh. This one's perfect! Black Rock Shooter!" Tya gets up and strikes a pose.

"I've never heard of her," I say, looking at the girl with a flaming blue eye and a dangerous look. "What's she from?"

"An anime of the same name. It's about a girl named Mato who is trying to help her friends ease their emotional pain and suffering. But in the process, she brings a girl in an alternate world to life."

"Black Rock Shooter?"

"Yeah. Black Rock Shooter uses her battles to get rid of everyone's pain in the real world. It's a good little series."

I think of all the hurt I've been through lately — the rape of my classmate, leaving my best friends, stress from always being so short of cash. It would be nice to have someone who dealt with all that. "I might like that anime."

"I'll send you the link." Tya pulls up a front, back, and side view of Black Rock Shooter. She's a black-haired girl with two mismatched ponytails, wearing a black, hooded jacket with a white star on the back. The jacket goes down to the middle of her calves but is completely open in the front, exposing her bikini top, belted black booty shorts, and knee-high boots. She has a giant gun and a blue glowing fire shape over her left eye. "This is going to be my cosplay!" Tya announces before eyeing me. "Don't be too offended by the skin content."

I put up my palm. "I don't care. I don't have to wear it."

Tya studies the pictures. "I hope I have enough time to pull this off. It's going to be tricky. Especially on a budget. I think my mom has some boots I can work with. She'll probably let me have them. I have the belts, the bikini top, and maybe some shorts that would work. Oh, and I think I have a black wig I can mess around with. The jacket I could probably get at the second-hand store and then fix up with my sewing machine."

"That gun looks pretty complex," I say. "And how are you going to pull off the glowing eye flame?"

"I could LED some clear plastic cut into flames for the eye. That way I can still see. The gun I'll build out of papier-mâché and then wire up with more LEDs." Tya taps her chin with her finger. "If I wear my Erza costume Friday, and my Porrim

Maryam costume from *Homestuck* on Sunday, I'll only have to build one costume. Perfect!" She pins me with her eyes. "Now, what are you going to wear?"

I pull my knees up to my chest, the bed sinking below me. "Uhh, can I wear my Batgirl costume?"

"You have a Batgirl costume?"

"Yeah. I wore it when I went to Edmonton Comic Expo with my friends Kaitlin and Cora last fall."

"And you dressed up?" Tya looks skeptical.

"Well, yeah."

"So why won't you dress up for Otafest?"

"Anime costumes are too skimpy," I say, a whine creeping into my voice.

"Oh, yeah, and comic costumes aren't? Besides, not all of them would have you showing a bunch of skin." Tya points her finger in the air. "We are getting you into anime cosplay." Tya types furiously and pulls up a picture of a girl with pink hair, pink bows, and a pink frilly dress. "You could be a magical girl!" she exclaims.

I shake my head, laughing. "You have to be kidding! No way. Try again."

"But I thought you wanted to dress like a girl," Tya says.

"Not that kind of girl. Jeez! Isn't there something less frilly?"

"Okay, okay, okay, okay." Tya types, snickering like she's up to something. "Here. How about this?"

I look at the anime version of a rocker chick with a corset top, miniskirt, and fishnet stockings. "Not on your life. What did I say about too much skin?" I have the feeling that Tya isn't taking this very seriously at all.

"Hmmm," she types in some words and hits enter. "Then this one would be perfect."

I shake my head, eyes tearing up from laughter. "I am not wearing a full suit of armor and I'm not playing a boy!"

"But Alphonse Elric is adorable," Tya says, batting her eyelashes.

"Still no. Anyway, I think I know who I want to be."

"Who?"

"Haruhi Fujioka from *Ouran High School Host Club*," I say, pulling up her picture.

Tya scrolls down and clicks on another picture. "In her bathing suit?"

I hit Tya with a pillow. "You perv. In her school uniform."

"The girl's one right?" she says picking another picture.

"Stop it. The blue jacket and black pants one." I find the picture I originally brought up of Haruhi in her boy's uniform, her short hair and eyes so like mine.

"But she's cross-dressing," Tya says.

I shake my head. "No, she's not. She's being Haruhi. Besides, she's still a girl and I like her."

"But what if someone thinks you're a guy?" Tya asks. "Won't that bother you?"

I think about Rose. If the rapist thought she was a guy, then she wouldn't have been attacked. Even if he didn't think she was a guy, but instead wasn't sure what gender she was, he probably wouldn't have bothered. And if that had happened, then Rose would still be in Fort McMurray, and so would I. "Actually, it might not be so bad," I say. "Besides, maybe I should try something new."

Tya grins. "Okay. Haruhi it is." Then she starts bouncing on her knees, almost making the laptop fall off the bed. "Ooh, what if you meet your Tamaki at Otafest? It could be a real romance!" She bats her eyes, holding her clutched hands by her cheek. "Think of the rose petals!"

I swat at her. "Stop. I told you, my mom won't let me date. Besides, I don't have time for a boyfriend. I have studying and babysitting, and *you*. If I met someone, one of those things would have to go."

"Ahh, you know you could never get rid of me!" Tya laughs. "Now let's look at what pieces we need for your costume."

"The jacket might be hardest thing to track down," I say. "I don't think the fashion industry has made baby blue sports jackets in a long time."

"Oh, hang on." Tya runs out of the room and comes back with a baby blue sports jacket. "My parents like to torture my bother. It might be too big for you but he wouldn't mind if you borrowed it." She smirks. "He'd love you if you lost it."

The jacket actually fits not too badly. It's supposed to be a little baggy. "I already have the white dress shirt, black dress pants, and shoes. Now all I need is a black tie I can paint."

"And I can help make the school logo!" Tya says getting on board. "Are you going to wear that all three days?"

"I could wear my Batgirl costume one of the days."

"I'm going to destroy you!" Tya laughs, attacking me with pillows. "You are so obsessed with superheroes!"

"Oh, *I'm* obsessed!" I laugh, attacking back. "Who's trying to make me go half-naked?"

"Otafest is going to be so much fun," Tya gasps through her giggles.

"I'm starting to think that," I reply.

★★★ CHAPTER NINE

TEMPTATION

Heavy books punch my back as I push open the public library doors. What Mr. Perez has against Wikipedia, I have no idea. Maybe he has ties to the publishing industry because every time we do a project he insists we use actual books instead of internet information. Luckily the C-Train runs right to the library. Also luckily, the library has manga and graphic novels, lots of them, so I can still read all my favourite stories even if they aren't current.

I adjust my backpack to stop it digging into my shoulders and head back onto the C-Train platform. It's warm today. A brisk wind is blowing from the mountains and melting the snow. Summer is nearly here. The C-Train comes and I ride the four stops from downtown to Kensington, where Mom works at the diner. I thought I'd pay her a visit and give her a little surprise.

The train pulls in five minutes later and I get off, brushing shoulders with a girl in a flower dress carrying a drum. Going down the stairs, across the tracks, and up the sidewalk I pass Another Dimension. I peer through the glass, heart picking up speed, as I try to catch a glimpse of Samir. I feel kind of bad for not going in. It's been three weeks, and I still haven't returned his comic, but babysitting and school have been keeping me busy. Maybe Mom was right about avoiding boys, but just because of the time commitment.

The thing is, a comic book shop is something I definitely need to avoid. Now that I babysit the boys regularly three times a week I have babysitting money, lots of it. I was paid today, and after taking out what I needed to pay Tya back for the Otafest ticket, I still have loads. I mean, I have decent willpower, but not comic book decent. So, fists clenched, I turn my eyes forward and keep walking, every fibre of my body wanting to head through the door, if only to breathe in the scent of ink, glossy paper, and Samir.

A sigh I can't control slips out of my lips.

Sadly, the store is on a corner and I have to pass yet another window of temptation. This one is filled with images of heroes, their eyes battle-hardened. They won't give one inch — and neither will I. I have a mission to accomplish and I will not fail. So I walk past Wonder Woman, Batman, and Black Canary with the pride of a fellow superhero.

Two blocks later, I open the door to the diner, the little silver bell tinkling out my arrival. The diner is pretty empty, just a hipster working on his laptop and a family eating at the far table. Mom looks up from the coffee machine and smiles. "Mariam! What are you doing here? Aren't you supposed to be at home studying?"

"I had to go to the library," I say, taking a seat at the counter, "and I have something for you."

"Oh, what's that?" she asks, coming over.

I zip open my backpack and pull out an envelope, handing it to my mom. She raises an eyebrow as she opens it. She has no idea this is coming. Excitement tingles through me. I try not to break out in a big grin.

"Mariam, what?" she pulls the two hundred and sixty dollars partway out of the envelope before sliding it back in and looking around. "Where did you get this?"

"Babysitting. It's my pay. I want you to have it. For rent or food or whatever."

"I . . . I . . ." Mom holds her hand to her chest, eyes clenching shut. "I can't take your money."

"It's our money. We need it right? Let me help."

"But I can't take it *all*."

I shrug. "I don't mind."

Her fingers flit through the envelope as the bell tinkles once more. A big guy walks in and sits at a nearby table. "Here." She shoves forty dollars back into my hand. "Take this. Get something for yourself at least."

"But . . ." I try to hand it back.

"Hey!" The guy snaps. "A little service?"

"Coming!" Mom calls out, a smile plastering her face. She turns back to me, hand covering mine. "You've earned it. Have fun."

I nod and spin on my stool to watch her serve the guy. He orders a coffee, black, and a burger with fries, slapping Mom's bottom as he finishes. "And make it snappy!"

Mom ignores his rudeness and explains how the coffee will be a minute as the pot was just started, then heads into the kitchen to give the cook the order. I glare at the guy. What I want to do is take the fork on his table and stab him in the gut, telling him to leave my mom alone and never come back. It's what Black Canary or Batgirl would do. Hurt him enough to scare him, but not enough to kill him.

What I actually do is sit there scowling until he looks at me and says, "What are you staring at? Think I'm sexy or something?" He chuckles at his own comment and cracks open his newspaper.

Mom returns and pours his coffee, taking it over to him. "Thanks, cutie." He winks, attempting to pinch her butt.

Mom moves too quick for him. She shakes her finger. "That's not allowed."

He laughs again. "But you're so damn cute!"

She walks away, not replying.

He keeps laughing. "Okay, okay. But we could always go on a date. Then I could show you some better moves."

My fists clench and I stand up. "I'm going to go," I say to my mom. "I'll see you at home."

She nods and says goodbye as she goes to clear the dishes from the table where the family has finished eating. I pass the guy, wanting to knock his coffee right into his lap. But I don't. I don't do anything. I just leave, the bell chiming my cowardice.

I have to walk back under the gaze of the superheroes on my way to the C-Train station. My heart burns. I hate that guy. I was so powerless. Mom seemed to handle things but even then, she still got slapped. It's just like the stuff she had to deal with back in Fort McMurray. Nothing has changed. Not as much as I would like. Guys are still pigs.

Maybe Haruhi was onto something. If that guy thought Mom was a boy, he wouldn't have acted that way. I'm starting to see the value in this whole cross-dressing thing.

I turn the corner, the door to the Another Dimension getting closer and closer. In my pocket, the forty bucks rubs between my fingers, slippery and tempting. I could just look. I wouldn't need to buy anything, or at least, I could limit myself to one comic, maybe two. Four at the most. It wouldn't be so bad. I just have to remember to save some money to buy a tie at the second-hand store to finish up my Haruhi costume.

Inside I take a deep breath, my anxiety and anger giving way to the rows and rows of comics. It's paradise. Literally paradise, and right away I feel so much better. I have a quick look around for Samir, but don't spot him. Then I remember, with a pang of disappointment, that it's Saturday, the day he doesn't work.

I walk through the Marvel section, picking up and putting down *A-Force, Deadpool,* and *She Hulk* in turn. I'm biding my time, because as much as I liked the *A-Force* Samir lent me, my heart will forever be in the DC camp.

Finally I head over to the DC aisles. There's someone else there too, looking through a *Teen Titans* comic. His dark hair still slightly messy. His body just as limber as the last time I saw him. His deep brown eyes sparkling behind his gold-rimmed glasses, as he thumbs through the pages. He looks up and smiles as he pauses. I smile too and quickly pick up a *Batgirl* comic, flipping through it, careful not to look like I was hoping he'd be here.

He closes his comic, adding it to the pile in his hands, before walking over to stand next to me. I concentrate hard on not looking at him, but, god, he's perfect. My heart pounds in my chest. My skin heats up. I duck my face away, hoping he doesn't see how red I know I've become. In my head I try to focus on working out how much it would cost to catch up with the *Batgirl* series. I'm really far behind. It will take nearly all my money.

"Hi, Mariam," Samir says, reaching out and picking out a *Batman* comic to add to the pile in his hands. "It's been a while."

The first place my mind goes is to how smooth his voice is. It throws my mind into a tailspin and makes me sound like an idiot. "Uh, yeah. I've been busy. You read *Batman*?"

"Like I said before, I'm more into the sidekicks. Red Robin in particular," he says, holding up his *Teen Titans* comic. "But Batman is the original."

"Yeah," I nod. "Red Robin is pretty awesome but I think I like Batgirl more."

He smiles. "Her new costume is pretty great."

"I love it!" I laugh. "I even made a version of it."

"I have a Red Robin costume myself." He blushes.

It's cute.

He looks around the store and sighs. "It would be so cool to be a real superhero."

My inability to do anything about the guy who slapped my mom still burns inside me. "I wish."

His eyes are far away as he adds, "It's just that sometimes, the world is so . . ."

I finger the money in my pocket. "Hard."

"Yeah," he nods. "Sometime escape is the only option. Thank god for comics, eh?"

I nod. "Exactly." It's like this guy — this really, really cute guy — is reading my mind. "Back in Fort McMurray, my friends and I used to practically live at the comic book shop."

"Oh, so you're not from Calgary?"

"No. I've been feeling a bit homesick but I have to say, when I'm in here, things just feel better."

Samir grins. "It was the same way with me. When I first moved here, I felt so lost. I was completely out of my element. But I liked comics and superheroes, so I stopped in and finally found something that didn't feel foreign. Besides, fans, no matter where they're from, are really welcoming people — even if they are a bit obsessed."

I laugh. "Not obsessed, committed."

"Some of them should be." Samir smirks.

"Have you ever been to a convention?" I ask.

"Yeah! You?"

"I've been to the Edmonton Comic Expo twice. I wanted to go to the Calgary one, since it's bigger, but I couldn't afford the ticket."

"Next year, you should come with me and my friends. We always have a good time."

A British accent calls from a few racks down. "Hey, Samir! Where are you?"

"Speaking of friends!" Samir throws up his hand and waves.

A girl with brown bobbed hair comes bouncing around the corner. "Oh! Found a fellow fan have you?" She smiles. "I'm Jemma."

"Mariam," I say.

"Nice to meet you. Are you another one of those Bat fanatics?" she asks, nodding to the *Batgirl* comic in my hand.

I laugh nervously. I'm not sure if she's being critical or just joking around.

She puts her hand to the side of her mouth and whispers, "It's okay, I'm totally into Beast Boy."

"Jemma, this is Mariam, the girl I gave that *A-Force* comic to," Samir says.

"Oh, yeah! What did you think of it?" Jemma asks.

"It was good." I nod. "I like the all-girl team-ups. Hang on, I'll grab it." I go to pull it out of my backpack.

Samir waves his hands. "No, no. Keep it. My gift to a fellow fan. It's not like I can't get more." He laughs.

Jemma looks at her phone. "Oh, jeez. We're late!" She gives me a wave. "Well it was nice meeting you, Mariam. Samir, get your stuff and let's go. We have to meet up with Fatima and Rintaro right away to work on my Colonel Mustang costume and your America costume for Otafest."

"You cosplay?" I ask.

"Well," Jemma says, throwing Samir a scowl, "I would if I could get Samir to focus on something other than Red Robin for more than two seconds. I mean he works here all day but somehow we still end up at the shop on his day off."

Samir shakes his head. "I forgot to get these yesterday," he complains to Jemma. "See you again?" he says to me.

"Probably," I smile. "I like this place."

"Cool." Samir grins, his feet shuffling.

I swear he blushes again.

"Yeah, yeah," Jemma says pushing him toward the till. "Come on! Costume time! We were late twenty minutes ago."

Samir laughs. "Bye, Mariam."

★★★ CHAPTER TEN

YOU'LL LOOK GREAT!

Tya, her sewing needle moving nimbly in her fingers, says, "Please tell me you got his phone number."

"No," I sigh.

"No photo either, huh?"

"That would have seemed a little stalkerish."

Tya grabs me by the shoulders, her needle threatening to prick me. "Mariam, you are so cute. There is no reason you shouldn't have a boyfriend."

"There are lots of reasons I shouldn't have a boyfriend, all of them starting with my mom. Besides, I don't even know if he's single. There was another girl with him you know."

Tya slumps down and goes back to sewing. "No excuses. Next time you meet a guy, get his number and maybe plan a date, huh? Especially if he looks like Tamaki."

I raise my eyebrow at her.

"Or Red Robin," she adds.

"I'll think about it. My mom is pretty strict. She doesn't like me hanging out with guys alone."

"So I'll come along!" Tya cheers.

"Oh, god." I shake my head.

"And . . . there!" She puts the finishing stitch into my Ouran Academy patch. It sits perfectly on the baby blue sports jacket.

"That looks amazing. You did a fantastic job." I run my fingers over the black, white, and gold crest, examining the near professional embroidering.

Tya shrugs, looking pleased. "It's what I do. Let's get into our costumes! I haven't seen you in yours yet and you haven't seen my finished product."

"Okay. I'll change in the bathroom," I say, grabbing my backpack and throwing the jacket over my arm.

"Good idea. That way there'll be no spoilers. See you in a few minutes."

I head to the bathroom and change into my costume, admiring myself in the mirror. I look just like Haruhi — short brown hair, white dress shirt, black tie with a purple stripe running down it, black dress pants and shoes, and the baby blue sports jacket with the Ouran Academy patch rounding everything out. Perfection.

I knock on Tya's door.

"*Ohairi*," she says.

I'm confronted with a blue, glowing flame coming out of Tya's left eye and a gun as big as my arm, also glowing blue, like it's about to shoot. All the tech distracts me from the sheer amount of skin Tya is showing off.

"Wow!" I say. "That gun is so . . . so . . ."

"Big," Tya finishes. "I know. My brother helped me light it up. Neat, huh? Thank goodness LEDs are cheap. Do you like the costume? It took me forever to get the wig to behave."

"I love it. You look just like Black Rock Shooter."

Tya walks all the way around me, nodding. "And you look like you just walked out of *Ouran High School Host Club*. Can I have a date?" she asks in her best Tamaki imitation.

"Ahh, no!" I say, acting like Haruhi. "Stop noticing me, *Senpai*!"

There's a knock on the door, and Tya's mom pops her head in. Her grin is as big and friendly as Tya's and her hair just as fluffy. "Hey, you girls are finished! You look great. What are you again?"

Tya groans, "Would it make a difference if I told you?"

Her mom laughs and shakes her head. "Probably not. I don't know any of those Japanese cartoons."

"Anime, Mom. It's anime. God. What do you want?" Tya asks.

"I just wanted to tell you the good news. I've booked our tickets! I even got a discount." Tya's mom claps.

"Tickets to what?" I ask.

Tya rolls her eyes. "One of my cousins in Jamaica is getting married and invited us to the wedding."

"Oh, don't be like that," Tya's mom scolds. "She's my sister's eldest and you two get along really well."

"When are you going?" I ask.

"May long weekend," Tya's mom says. "It can't come soon enough for me."

"Wait! What?" All the colour drains from Tya's face. "I can't go!"

Tya's mom frowns. "What are you talking about? Of course you can go. It's been planned for months."

"You never said when it was!" Tya shouts, tears already forming in her eyes.

"You never asked."

"But that's Otafest!"

"Well you'll have to miss it," Tya's mom states.

"But my costume . . . Mom, I . . ." Tya stops talking, over-whelmed with emotion.

"I'm sorry, Tya." Her mom uses the back of her finger to wipe away a tear. "But I don't think Shandee will change the wedding date because of a cartoon festival."

"Anime, Mom!" Tya yells.

"Anime. Whatever." Tya's mom throws up her hands. "Still. We're going. Now I have to talk to your dad. We can discuss this later." She closes the door behind her.

Tears streaming, Tya collapses on the bed. "Everyone was going to love this costume. They were going to be so impressed. I worked so hard. And now, no one will see it, unless . . ." Tya eyes me, her attitude going from depressed to diamond.

"Oh, no," I say crossing my arms and backing away.

Tya jumps up and grabs my shoulders. "We're the same size and you would look perfect in this!"

"It's a bikini!" I protest.

"Exactly. Just like at the beach, no big deal. Come on. I worked so hard. I can't stand the thought of it sitting in the closet until the next con."

"I'll freeze."

"It has a jacket."

"I'll look stupid."

"Do I look stupid?"

"No," I admit. Tya actually looks like a prostitute. Or she would if she ditched the jacket, wig, and big glowing gun.

"Come on," Tya pleads. "Wear it Friday, for a couple of hours, just long enough for people to see it."

My mom's disapproval of the strip-club girls and floozies, as she calls them, back in Fort McMurray runs through my mind. So does the big talk about self-respect and self-protection. I bow my head. I would be letting Mom down if I said yes.

Tya takes my arm, tears starting to fall again. "I'll die if this costume doesn't go to Otafest. It's not fair. I've worked so hard. Please."

I would be letting Tya down if I said no.

My teeth play over my bottom lip as I weigh my options. Mom won't let me go to something like Otafest alone. But Samir and Jemma said they were going so, that's kind of like going with someone. Plus Tya did put a lot of work into the costume. Still, the exposed belly and chest, the sheer amount of leg . . . Mom wouldn't want me to be eye candy for a bunch of drooling fanboys. Then again, Tya says people at Otafest dress up. They're showing their love for their favourite characters, not trying to get a date. But the costume is so skimpy. Mom is going to worry I'll get assaulted and I know how dangerous men can be. Then again, this is Otafest not Fort McMurray or the diner. Maybe I'm freaking out about nothing. Arrgh! This is so hard.

"Please?" Tya whispers. "At least get a picture by the rock they always paint up for Otafest. That would only take a minute. One minute."

Anxiety flutters through my chest. Panic clutches my throat. Then I realize one more thing. "I don't even know where that is! I don't know my way around the University of Calgary."

"It's by cosplay hill, where everyone hangs out. It will be easy to spot. Trust me." Tya tries to smile, her tears still shining on her cheeks.

"But . . ." I'm shaking.

Tya whispers one last please.

I take a deep breath. Black Rock Shooter's entire goal is to take people's emotional suffering and ease it. Wearing the Black Rock Shooter costume would ease Tya's emotional pain. It's a real way to be the superhero I've always dreamed of being, not just a pretend one. And Mom taught me to be there for my friends and family, so she shouldn't really mind. It's only going to be the one time. Just a quick picture, nothing more. I can manage that. "Okay," I finally say.

Tya's face splits in the biggest smile I've ever seen. She jumps up and wraps me in a hug. "Oh, thank you, Mariam. Thank you a million times." She holds me at arm's length. "You'll look great!"

My eyes focus on Tya's bellybutton, out for the world to see. I shudder. "I hope so," I reply.

CHAPTER ELEVEN

PROMISES

The more I think about what I've agreed to do, the more panicky I become. I want to help Tya but every time I think of that costume, my pulse quickens and I feel faint. "I need my mom," I finally whisper to myself.

She's working at the diner again. The ninth day in a row. It's getting a little ridiculous. Still, with overtime and my contribution, rent will be a breeze. We might even be able to start making headway on some of our debts.

But I wish she was home more.

Watching Calgary out the window of the C-Train, I remember the first time Kaitlin took Cora and me to the Edmonton Comic Expo and my mom tried "help" with my Supergirl costume. I thought it would be good idea to ask her to sew it for me since she's an awesome seamstress. But she made the skirt ankle-length and bought pink fabric for the cape because it was on sale. It was Grandma Poitras who helped me fix it up just in time for the trip. She cut the skirt to my knees and dyed the cape red. Thank goodness she's such a fangirl. Still, it was pretty funny, that ankle-length Supergirl costume with its pink cape. Classic mom. Her "close enough" was always good for a laugh.

My grin reflects back at me in the glass.

I know she'll tell me what to do about Tya's Black Rock Shooter costume. I mean, she might hate the idea of it. She might tell me I can't go. If that happens, Tya can't blame me. It wouldn't be my fault. I have to listen to my mom, right? Then again, Mom might think the costume isn't that bad. Tya is kind of right about it being like a bikini. Actually, with the jacket, it's even more covered up than a bikini, so Mom might not have any issues with the whole thing. Either way, Mom will know what to do.

I still think I'll leave out the part about Tya not going. Mom is too jumpy about that kind of stuff. I'll just say that Tya made two costumes and she wants to show off both. That should work. It's not such a big deal. I mean, I know I can handle the convention. It's just the costume that has me rattled.

I get off the train and walk by the comic shop, trying not to peek in. I know Samir works today, but it's not why I'm here. Besides, I'm broke again. There is no real reason to go in. Even if I actually want to.

Walking past the art store, t-shirt shop, and smoothie place my stomach gets more and more tense. I wonder if I should even be doing this. Mom's been getting more anxious since we moved to Calgary, not less, as Kaitlin assured me she would. She's even getting picky about me taking public transit alone, though I have told her repeatedly that the library still refuses to come to me. And bringing up any talk about looking for a job makes her lose her mind.

I *know* she's not going to like the costume. I don't need to ask. I wonder if I'm really doing this so I can get out of it. Some superhero I am. Trying to weasel out of a promise by using my mom. That is such a cowardly thing to do.

I stop walking. The diner window is right beside me but I make no move to enter. I just stand there and think of the look on Tya's face when I tell her my mom said no to the costume. It's a mean way of doing it. If I really don't want to wear the stupid thing, I should just say so and not make others do my dirty work. I mean, I keep telling Mom how I'm almost seventeen and I should be treated like an adult. I guess I should live by those words and start acting like one.

Beginning with making my own decisions.

While I stand there, debating with myself, the jerk who slapped my mom's butt last time pushes his way into the diner. He bumps into a hipster guy and his girlfriend trying to exit. The hipster yells in surprise. The jerk sticks his finger in the hipster's face. The hipster puts up his hands, palms out, and backs away. The jerk throws his chest forward, spit flying from his mouth as he yells, a fist forming next to his hip. Mom scurries to intervene. She sweet-talks the jerk, her hands flitting on his shoulders. The hipster and his girlfriend open the door and scurry out, looking relieved. My mom pulls out a chair for the jerk, hands him a newspaper, and pours him a coffee. He slaps her butt. She takes it. She doesn't do anything to stop him. Not even when he puts his hand on the small of her back to give his order, fingers clenching.

I shudder. It's gross. She should stop him. Tell him to leave. Or I should.

But I'm frozen. Again. Too angry or scared, or both, to do anything but turn and run back down the street. I want to help her but I don't know how. Grandma Poitras didn't cover this kind of stuff in her self-defense training. What should I do? What should Mom do? Is it easier to just let him have his way?

Is that what she's doing? Taking the easy path? The coward's way out?

I clench my teeth. That won't be me. I'm no coward. I gave Tya my word. It doesn't matter that I'm scared. I'll wear her costume. I'll wear it with pride. I'm going to . . . I slow down, legs shaking, breath coming in gasps. I feel weak and overwhelmed. I want to be somewhere safe. I turn the corner, wobble up to the comic book shop, pull open the door, fill my lungs with ink and paper, my hand gripping the wall.

"Hey, Mariam. You okay?" Samir is at the till, flipping through a graphic novel. He comes around the counter and takes my elbow. "Something happen?"

I shake my head and steady my breathing. "No, I'm fine. I just wanted . . ." I look around.

"Yeah. Got you." He nods. "Browse away. It's been pretty slow today. I was going to throw on the *Son of Batman* movie. Want to watch with me?"

He gives me a gentle smile, stepping back and giving me my space. My anxiety, anger, fear, unease, all melt away under his gaze.

"Yeah," I say. "Thanks."

We sit on stools behind the counter watching the movie, talking about how unrealistic Talia's heels are when all the male assassins are wearing ninja shoes, and intermittently helping customers. I load up a ten-year-old girl looking for some 'real heroes' with *Gotham Academy*, *She Hulk*, and the *Amulet* series while Samir shows her brothers the *Asterix* and *Tin Tin* comics they request. We put the new order of t-shirts on hangers, and I label customer orders, while Samir calls them. The movie plays in the background. Finally the credits come on.

"Thanks for the help," Samir says, taking out the disk and throwing in some *Young Justice* as a replacement.

"I wish I could work here for real," I say.

"Yeah, that would be awesome. I'll let you know if there's ever a job opening. Right now, there's nothing."

I shrug. "That's okay. My mom doesn't want me to work a real job."

"Yeah, my mom is overprotective too. Luckily my dad sides with me a lot."

"I don't have a dad," I say, my teeth clenching and a knot growing in my chest. "My parents are divorced. Dad ditched us for a twenty-year-old cook he met at the oilfield work camp. I haven't seen him in years."

"Well," Samir says, "then it's lucky your mom has you."

"I guess," I say, thinking of that jerk grabbing at Mom and my inability to do anything to stop it. "I don't know how much I help."

"I'm sure you're great. I mean you seem really great." Samir blushes and turns away to do some sudden arranging of the bobbleheads on the counter. "Anyway, I should get back to work."

"Uh, yeah. I have a ton of homework," I reply. "Thanks again."

I leave feeling a lot better than when I went in. I know what to do now. Wear the costume. Be the hero. Make Tya happy. As for Mom and her issues, I guess I'll have to think about that a bit more. But there must be some solution. I'm just not sure what it is.

★★★

Tya packs up the last of the costume, folded carefully in a plastic bag. "Look after this," she tells me. "I want to wear it the next chance I get."

"Why don't you just wait then?" I ask. I'm still not completely comfortable with the whole idea.

"Are you trying to back out?" Tya asks, winking.

"No!" I say. "Of course not. I said I would do it."

"That's what I like about you. You're loyal." Tya hovers the wig over my head. "Ohh! You're going to look so cute in this! I can't wait to see it. Make sure you take lots of photos. And pose with everyone who asks. I want a million pictures all over the internet."

I shiver, like I've swallowed a bucket of ice. "All . . . over . . . the . . ."

"Think viral!" Tya beams. "What if Jessica Merizan wants a photo? If she does, you *have* to tell her I made the costume. Ohhh!" Tya squeals. "I am so jealous."

"Jessica who?"

"Jessica Merizan, she's a famous cosplayer who's going to be there. A pro. She has her own webshow and she was even on *Heroes of Cosplay*. She's amazing! I want to be like her one day."

"A professional cosplayer?"

"No!" Tya says, hands on her hips. "I want to do more than that. I want to make costumes for people who cosplay, and original costumes for movies and plays and stuff. One day, everyone will know my name! But right now, I'll settle for Otafest. Do me proud, Mariam, my entire future hangs on your shoulders. Literally."

"No pressure, huh?" I gulp.

"None," Tya laughs. "And just think of it. On Saturday and Sunday you get to be boring old Haruhi, unless . . ."

"What?" I ask.

"You meet a Tamaki cosplayer. Then there can be fireworks!"

"Not this again," I groan. "I told you —"

"Yeah, yeah, you're not allowed to date. I know. But it's not a date if you both just *happen* to be at the same event. If you do meet a Tamaki, I want pictures! And details! And a wedding invitation! Oh, and you have to name your first born after me."

"Stop!" I give her a playful push.

"But I'm right, yeah?" Tya nudges me, laughing.

"Maybe," I admit. "It would be cool to meet Tamaki in the flesh. But right now, I'll just be happy to make it through Friday."

She pats my back. "You'll be fine. Besides, you like Black Rock Shooter, don't you?"

I did watch the series, and I really did like the character. Even more so, I liked the animation. The way Black Rock Shooter moved like an acrobat, the grit of determination on her face, how she focused herself before every attack. It was amazing. The writing was good too. The whole thing had me hooked to the end.

"Yeah." I smile. "I do, and I won't let you down." I make a fist and hold it near my face. "I will take your suffering for you."

"And I will be suffering," Tya sighs, "knowing you're at Otafest, while I'm watching a stupid wedding."

"In Jamaica. Come on. Sun, sand, beach. You can't complain that much."

"Want to bet? I'm pretty good at complaining."

"That you are!" her mom says, coming into the room. "Are you packed, Tya?"

"Yup. I'm ready to go. I'm just giving Mariam the costume," Tya says.

Her mom gives me a quick hug. "It's so nice of you to do this for Tya. She was so upset about her costume. You're a really good friend."

"Thanks," I say, guilt crawling through me at the thought of nearly telling my mom about the whole thing. What would they think about me if I couldn't do this?

At least I made the right decision.

"You're ready to go!" Tya says, handing me the bag and the giant gun. "The switch for the lights is there and the battery pack is there. I put an extra set of batteries in the bag in case you run out of juice. Thanks again for doing this! You're the best friend in the world."

"No problem!" I say, beaming, my worry slipping away under all the praise.

CHAPTER TWELVE

AMERICA IS ALWAYS THE HERO

I don't feel like a hero. I feel like a fraud.

I'm going to a place I've never been to. To a convention I know almost nothing about. In a costume that shows off more skin than I'm even remotely comfortable with and Tya is texting me the message, *Excited yet???*

Maybe I can pretend I'm sick. I certainly feel sick. My stomach is doing flips, my head pounds, and my mouth is as gritty as a Popsicle dropped on the beach. I finger the folded costume's silky fabric hidden in my backpack. Everything is ready to go.

Except me.

I take a deep breath. Think of Batgirl. If she gives her word, she keeps it. So does Haruhi. She's a loyal as they get. Black Rock Shooter wouldn't run. She never runs. So why is Mariam so wimpy?

I shove my Otafest ticket in my backpack, sling the giant gun over my shoulder, and push my fears away. Actually, with the gun, I feel kind of badass. Maybe I can manage — at least for a while.

I scout the apartment. Mom is still in the bathroom,

having just come home from her shift. Perfect. Walking lightly, I take the gun and my backpack to the front door and open it silently, slipping the weapon outside. Closing the door silently once more, I yell towards the bathroom. "Okay, Mom, I'm going. I have my phone if you need to call me."

Mom comes out, hairbrush in hand. "I thought you and Tya were going together. Isn't she meeting you here?"

I bite my lip. This is the tricky part. "Tya is meeting me down there," I say, keeping a super casual tone to my voice.

Mom looks concerned. "I don't know if I'm comfortable with that. You should probably go together. Maybe call her." Mom motions to my phone.

I sigh. "Mom, I'm nearly seventeen. I think I can handle being alone for short periods of time."

"Still," Mom presses. "I would feel happier if you were together."

Angry heat creeps up my neck. Why can't she trust me? I'm supposed to be practicing being an adult. If Mom wanted a real, honest relationship, she would give me more freedom.

These lies are on her.

I fix my story. "Jeez, Mom! I'm not meeting Tya down at the university! We're meeting at the C-Train station. We're going together from there. What did you think?"

Mom studies at me for what feels like minutes. Long minutes. Like she isn't believing one word. But in the end, she smiles. "Okay, have a good time, and be careful."

I turn and head out the door, held breath escaping from my lips. That was close.

★★★

The C-Train flows into downtown with its glimmering lights and silvery buildings. At every stop my courage ebbs away. At every stop I get closer to wearing a bikini in front of hundreds of people. My heart beats louder in my ears, my chest aches, and I have to talk myself back into the plan over and over again. It's less and less effective every time.

Soon downtown vanishes and the Bow River appears as the train glides north over the bridge to Kensington. Finally, unable to justify my decision a minute longer, I stand. It's not my stop but I'm getting off and going home. Tya can be mad. Tya can hate me. She can say I'm the worst friend in the world. I don't care. I can't do this. I can't . . .

"Hey! Mariam, is that you?" A familiar voice pulls me out of my head. It sounds like Samir but when I look towards the speaker I don't recognize the person who's talking. The guy has gold-rimmed glasses, blonde hair, khaki cargo pants, and a bomber jacket with a star on the left breast. Still something strikes me as familiar about his caramel-coloured skin, brown eyes, and long black lashes, but I can't quite put the image to the voice.

He laughs. "Sorry, you probably don't recognize me like this." He pulls off his wig, revealing short black hair.

"Samir! It is you!" I exclaim, a warm rush filling my chest and making me blush.

"Yeah," he chuckles. "I'm America. Did the wig throw you off?"

"A little," I admit. "You're a character from *Hetalia*, right? That political anime where all the countries are people?" I ask, showing off some of my newfound knowledge and thankful that Tya was so insistent I watch lots of shows.

"Exactly! Are you going to Otafest too?"

I sit on the bench across from him. My stomach full of butterflies calms their fluttering. "Yeah," I say.

He looks over what I'm wearing, eyes falling on my prop. "Nice gun."

I pat my giant firearm. "Thanks."

His forehead creases in thought, then his eyes crinkle in a grin. "You're not going to dress up as Black Rock Shooter, are you?"

I nod, not admitting that I nearly chickened out.

"That is really cool," Samir gushes. "I'd love to see that. She's a great character even if the anime is kind of dark. I mean, the whole idea of taking on others' pain by basically pit fighting every day is a little intense."

"Yeah." I nod. "But in the end everyone learns to accept their own pain, leaving behind a much different world. So it's all good."

Samir smiles. "That's true. Still, dark though."

I shrug. "This actually isn't my costume. I'm wearing it for a friend. Tya."

"Oh, the one who was looking for the *Otomen* manga?"

"That's the one."

"Why couldn't she wear it?"

"Her parents made her go to a wedding in Jamaica," I explain.

Samir fakes a sad look. "Poor her."

"I know. Heartbreaking." I roll my eyes.

"Are you going to be Black Rock Shooter all weekend?"

I shake my head. "No. Tomorrow I'm wearing my Haruhi Fujioka costume."

"Nice! *Ouran High School Host Club*. That's a great anime." Samir asks, "Is this your first time at Otafest?"

83

I nod. "I'm a little nervous. I don't know where to go."

"Oh, that part is easy," Samir says. "I'll show you."

"My hero," I tease.

Samir slides his wig back on and gives me a wink. "America is always the hero."

We arrive at University Station and the platform fills with cosplayers leaving the C-Train. We follow a Pikachu and a girl dressed as Russia, also from *Hetalia*, who gives Samir a smile and a wave of her prop, a piece of pipe covered in fake blood.

"Do you know her?" I ask.

"No. But we're in the same fandom. Everyone here is really friendly. You're going to love it," Samir says.

He takes me past the Biology building and along the Science buildings, pointing out the doors I'll use for things like the anime music video room and the screening rooms. He tells me where most of the panels are held and shows me the many signs and chalk markings on the ground pointing every which way. We pass a hill full people dancing to vocaloid music in cosplay. The energy is catchy. I feel immediately at home. My cheeks spread in a grin.

"Fun, huh?" Samir says. "There's the place your friend was talking about." He points to a rock painted with the Triforce from the *Legend of Zelda* video games. "They paint the rock different every Otafest. Nice choice for this year."

A girl runs over to the rock with her friend and poses on it, flashing the double peace sign. My nerves start up again. Soon I'll have to do that, in booty shorts and a bikini top. I bite my lip and clutch my gun. *Black Rock Shooter never runs*, I remind myself.

"Through those doors is where you get your wristband. You'll have to get that weapon checked at the props table. It will be right by the check-in table."

"It doesn't actually fire," I joke.

"Then you should be fine," Samir chuckles. "Here, let me give you my phone number so we can find each other easier." He gives me his number and I give him mine. "Nice phone," he laughs. "It's actually older than mine. I didn't think that was possible."

"Yeah," I smile. "Hand me downs."

"Don't I know it," Samir says. "Anyway, this is a really safe place," he tells me, "but it's still better to stay in groups, more fun, too. So, if you want, call me once you're checked in and I'll tell you where my friends and I are. We can . . ." I swear he gets a little pink. "Hang out or . . . you know, whatever."

"Okay," I say, certain I'm turning a bit pink too.

"Oh, and there's an Otafest info-line too. If you ever find yourself lost or confused or even in trouble, give them a call. They'll help."

"Thanks for helping me." I say.

"I told you, America is always the hero." He raises his hand, looking every bit like the super-confident character he's play-ing. "See you around the con I hope!"

★★★ CHAPTER THIRTEEN

I AM BLACK ROCK SHOOTER

In the cramped bathroom stall I do up the bow on the front of the bikini top. Luckily I'm fairly flat chested like Black Rock Shooter, nothing to fall out or go astray, unlike Tya. Before I lose my nerve I slip on the jacket and do up the ties at my throat. It covers my butt, thankfully, but nothing in the front. My entire torso is out for all to see. The shorts are *short*. Way shorter than anything I would ever choose to wear. And my thighs, bare from the knee up, feel really exposed.

Stuffing my civilian clothes into my backpack, I head out of the stall and over to the counter where I put my wig on, standing between two other girls who are also adjusting and primping. One of them is pink-haired Sakura from *Naruto* in a red dress with white trim. The other is a blue-haired schoolgirl from an anime I'm not familiar with. They both look great.

I pull on my wig, attach the glowing blue eye piece, then put on black gloves, making sure my Otafest wristband is still visible. Now I have a problem. Between my gun and my backpack, my hands are full, and besides, I can't carry around my backpack the entire time without ruining the look of the outfit.

"Um, excuse me?" I ask, my voice so quiet I wonder if anyone can hear it.

The girl dressed as Sakura smiles. "What's up?" she asks with a light British accent.

"Is there a coat check around here or something?" I hold up my backpack.

She nods. "I'm heading there next. You can come with me."

I puff out a sigh of relief.

The girl dressed as Sakura studies me. "Hey, aren't you that girl from the comic book shop. Batgirl fan, right?"

I nod, not recognizing Sakura as anyone I've ever met. "Uh, sorry, I don't . . ."

She laughs, "Beast Boy fan. Jemma in real life."

"Wow, really?" I ask. "I never would have guessed. Are you meeting Samir?"

"Oh, I'll probably run into him at some point. I'm actually here with some other friends right now. You look amazing by the way," Jemma says, touching my jacket. "So authentic."

I peer in the mirror and give myself a good look. What gazes back at me from the smudged surface is Black Rock Shooter, no doubt about it. Tya wasn't kidding when she said I looked like her. I touch my belly and so does the image of Black Rock Shooter. "It's not me," I whisper. "I'm her."

"Pardon?" Jemma asks.

"Um . . ." I blush at being caught talking to myself. "It's not mine, the costume, my friend made it. She couldn't come, so I'm wearing it for her."

"She made this?" Jemma runs her fingers over the white star on the back of the black jacket and then over the one on the left of my chest. "But these are embroidered. The boots are even exact. She didn't buy any of it?"

"I think she might have gotten some of the basic stuff at a thrift shop and changed it up," I say, "but she didn't buy anything pre-made."

The blue-haired schoolgirl shakes her head. "She did an amazing job."

"Pass on my congratulations," Jemma adds.

"I will, thanks!" I smile, looking forward to the conversation with Tya later tonight. She's going to be so happy.

I follow Jemma out of the registration building to another building where we stash our backpacks and coats. Luckily the shorts have enough of a pocket to hold my phone. This is one of the few times I'm glad my phone is such a piece of junk. It's small and can fit just about anywhere.

I thank Jemma and head outside again following the sound of music, swaying in my high-heeled boots. More and more people are arriving. I'm impressed by how much my anime knowledge has grown thanks to Tya. I actually recognize about twenty percent of the costumes. I see a whole basketball team from an anime whose name I've forgotten as well as a bunch of people being countries from *Hetalia*. There are people dressed as imaginary animals, demons, and schoolgirls. The *Homestuck* fandom makes a big showing with their grey skin and orange-yellow horns. I even see Iron Man and Deadpool. Mind you, Deadpool does tend to be everywhere.

The closer I get to cosplay hill the busier it gets. I hear a whistle, but I don't know if it's directed at me. I picture myself as I was in the mirror. I am the dangerous and deadly Black Rock Shooter, saviour of all in pain, not Mariam. I grip my gun tight. Hold it up. Show off the LED lights. Black Rock Shooter is here! Let the show begin!

Someone taps my shoulder and I jump, shrieking.

"Sorry!" a girl dressed as a My Little Pony exclaims — hoof hovering over her mouth. "I wanted to ask if I could take your picture. That's an amazing costume."

I nod, pose, and try to look as awesome as possible.

"Oooh, Black Rock Shooter! Love it!" another person says. "Can I have a photo too?"

In all, twelve or so people take photos and I pose with another five before I finally get moving again. My nerves go silent. What people are seeing isn't me, or my skin. They're seeing Tya's workmanship bringing a character they admire to life.

With confidence I head over to the rock Samir pointed out to me. No one is posing on it. I lean against its cool painted surface and pull out my phone, trying to take a selfie. It doesn't really work. I can only get my head and shoulders in the shot. I know Tya wants the whole thing. Proof that I was there and a way to show off her costume online. I don't know how I'm going to do this.

"Can I help?" a guy dressed as the blonde and elegant Tamaki Suoh from *Ouran High School Host Club* says, twirling a rose in his fingers as he winks at me. Heat flushes into my face and a giggle bubbles forth before I can stop it.

I compose myself as fast as I can. I really like *Ouran High School Host Club*, and Tamaki Suoh in real life is super sexy. For a moment I'm lost in my fandom. After all, if you don't count Red Robin and maybe Superboy, Tamaki is my favorite animated crush. Not to mention he is the guy I'm supposed to be in love with when I play Haruhi tomorrow. My hands start to sweat. My heart beats louder. I grin. He grins back.

"So, princess . . ." he says, his voice like silk.

"It would be great if you could help," I say with a blush. "I'm having trouble getting a picture of myself." I realize

I sound completely self-centred and try to babble out an explanation about Tya and the costume.

But he stops me midsentence with a finger to my lips and smiles in that perfect Tamaki way, replying, "I would be honoured to take your picture." He slips the phone from my fingers with a bow, while saying, "You look divine." Then he gets me to pose first with my gun down, relaxed, then in battle mode, gun pointed at him. He tells me to move in front of a modern art sculpture and takes some pictures there, posing in a kneeling position and another where I'm looking off into the distance. He even does a close-up of me looking like I'm going to pull my enemies guts out with my bare hands. As he takes the pictures he throws out all kinds of compliments like "A photo can't capture your true beauty, my princess," and "Your eyes sparkle like angels live in them." So before long, I'm blushing all over again.

When we're done I look through the photos. He has talent. "Thanks," I say. "These are really nice."

"It's hard not to take a nice picture when the subject is you."

I look at my feet, my face on fire.

He chuckles. It sounds just like the anime. "Now that I've helped you," he says, holding out his hand in a perfect imitation of Tamaki, "would you indulge me with a dance, my princess?"

I nod, shyness flooding over me. Tamaki wants to dance . . . with me. Eeep!

★★★ CHAPTER FOURTEEN

PRINCESS

Tamaki leads me up onto cosplay hill where one of the theme songs from *Soul Eater* is playing. I dance, a little awkwardly in the heels. Nearby, a couple of *Fairy Tail* cosplayers dance and laugh, one of them dressed as Lucy Heartfilia, with her whip and celestial keys, and the other playing Grey Fullbuster. Grey is shirtless, as usual, dressed only in belted jeans and boots, which is more than what he often wears in the anime and manga. As I recall, he has a terrible tendency to strip down to his boxers ever since his teacher made him train that way. Now it's a bad habit he can't seem to break. I'm happy that I'm in absolutely no danger of really seeing Grey naked here. The two cosplayers give me a thumbs up and smile. I wave back as another girl shimmies up to Grey and unzips his pants, hooting, "Strip, Grey, Strip!"

Grey pulls away, his smile disappearing as he pushes her off. "Stop!" he yells. "Leave me alone!"

"Oh, come on!" Tamaki whoops, laughing. "Give yourself to her!"

"Yeah!" the girl says, reaching in again. "Give yourself to me."

"Stop it!" I say. "We need to help him!" Before the words are even completely out of my mouth an Otafest volunteer has already put himself between the girl and Grey. He motions for her to follow him down the hill as two more volunteers arrive, one talking into a radio, the other speaking to Grey, notepad out.

"His loss," Tamaki says, turning his attention back to me. "I wouldn't object."

I frown. "But he shouldn't be treated that way."

"Yeah, if he were a girl I'd agree, but he's a guy, the rules are different."

"No, they're not!"

Tamaki shrugs. "You don't think he should be flattered by the attention?"

"Not that kind of attention."

Tamaki bows, his arms sweeping. "Well then, fair lady, I surrender to your opinion. After all," his eyes scrunch up with pleasure, "it's not worth fighting about when we have much more interesting things to discuss."

"*Senpai*!" a group of voices call out. "There you are!"

Tamaki is attacked by a whole bunch of boys in Ouran Academy uniforms. I look around, stunned. It's like I've fallen into the actual anime. There's Honey, with his toy rabbit. Kyoya, holding his notepad and pen while pushing up his glasses. Hikaru and Kaoru Hitachiin, who actually look like they might be twins in real life, and a guy playing Mori, who towers over everyone, grim, silent, and kind of intimidating.

"Wow, you have everyone," I say, impressed.

Tamaki shakes his head, heaving a deep sigh. "We are one short. My beautiful Haruhi is missing."

"Missing?" I ask, looking around to see if their absent

cosplay friend is within sight. "Did you lose her?"

"No." The boy playing Kyoya corrects me. "We didn't have anyone to play her."

Tamaki looks away, his eyes practically sparkling. "Sadly, we are incomplete."

I laugh.

He looks hurt.

"No, sorry," I say, waving my hand. "I just meant, I'm planning on playing Haruhi tomorrow. I have the costume all ready to go. I'm wearing this costume today because my friend couldn't make it to Otafest and she wanted me to show it off."

"Well, you're doing a magnificent job!" one of the twins says, eyeing me and nudging his brother. I'm not sure if it's Hikaru or Kaoru — they've done such a good job at creating their costumes to be alike.

Tamaki shoots them a look, just like the real Tamaki would.

"Sorry boss," they say together.

I stick out my hand. "I'm Mariam," I say.

"René Tamaki Richard de Grantaine Suoh," Tamaki says in return, kissing it.

The kid playing Honey sighs, "His name is Rick. I'm Lee." Lee is shorter than everyone else and looks like he might actually be a little brother to one of them, rather than a high schooler like the rest of us.

Rick scowls, snapping, "I told you, call me Tamaki this weekend."

"Of course, *Senpai*," the guy playing Kyoya says, scowling at Lee. "I'm Tobias. It's nice to meet you."

The twins Hikaru and Kaoru box me in, each grabbing a hand and shaking.

"I'm Sung-Hyun." One smiles.

"I'm Hyun-Min." The other grins. "But you can call me Hyun and him Sung. That's what everyone else does.

"Are you really twins?" I ask.

"Really and truly," Sung says.

"He's always wearing my face," Hyun jokes.

Mori finally introduces himself as Paul in a quiet voice, his face a little flushed.

Rick strokes his chin in a very Tamaki-like way, as if considering something. "You should hang out with us tomorrow. You could be our missing piece. And," he leans in, his eyes almost shimmering, "it would make me truly happy."

"Yeah!" Sung and Hyun say in unison. "That would be fun!"

I look around. There are so many people. Samir was right, it's probably better if I hang out in a group. Besides, these guys seem really nice. "Okay."

The twins high-five.

"Where and when should I meet you?" I ask.

"How about here?" Tobias suggests, "At ten o'clock we're doing an Ouran photo shoot."

"A real photo shoot?" I ask, impressed.

Hyun nods. "Rick paid for it himself. He wants to make sure we have photos to pass out to our fans."

"The cost was substantial," Rick says, waving his hand. "But our Ouran Host Club exists to bring fortune to the ladies. So I don't mind footing the bill."

Sung and Hyun lean into one another and chime, "The ladies love us."

Rick cups my cheek in his hand while holding his rose against my other, petals brushing my lips. "Will you join us?" he asks in that silky Tamaki voice. "With you we will be complete." His eyes sparkle again and I envision petals falling from the sky.

"You really want me there?" I ask, barely believing this is all real.

"We would be lost without you, princess," he replies.

My cheeks heat up. "Okay. It sounds like fun." I giggle. Rick is so awesome.

Being close, I notice he's not wearing a wig. Rick has actually dyed his hair blond and had it cut just like the character. His face is coated with a light foundation to cover his tan skin and he's wearing violet contacts to hide what I'm assuming are brown eyes. If it weren't for his slightly rounder face and the shape of his eyes, he really could be a living Tamaki. I give Rick my phone number so we can contact each other for the rest of the con, then he says, "Now, let's see what kind of trouble we can stir up."

"Well," I say looking at the schedule, "I was thinking of going to see a panel on *Hetalia* then another on how to make bento lunches. I want to surprise my friend Tya when she gets back from her trip."

"But, my lovely princess," Rick waves his finger at me. "Those panels are so pedestrian. The panels we are seeing will enlighten even the commonest of commoner. And besides," he falls to one knee and takes my hand in his. "I can't be without you, now that we have found each other."

I think of my options. I could sit alone at a panel or hang out with Tamaki Suoh. Besides, there's another *Hetalia* panel tomorrow I can see instead, and he's just so charming!

"How can I resist?" I say, still holding his hand as he stands.

He smiles and pulls me close. "Perfect."

★ ★ ★ CHAPTER FIFTEEN

GUILT

"So, how was it?" Mom asks as I walk in the door. It's half past ten and she looks tired. I know she waited up for me.

Silently I let the gun slip from my hand against the wall outside the apartment. There will be no sneaking it to my room right now. I hope that it will still be there by the time Mom goes to bed.

"It was amazing!" I say, shutting the door behind me and taking off my shoes. "There were so many people and costumes. It was the best thing ever." I sink into a chair at the table.

"So you managed to meet up with Tya?" Mom fills the kettle with water and turns it on, preparing to make tea.

My chest twinges with guilt. "Oh, yeah. No problem."

I hate to lie, but I was totally safe. Everyone was amazingly nice. I met up with Samir, talked to tons of people, and made lots of friends. I even found my Tamaki, just like Tya said. In fact I found the entire Host Club. And I have plans for tomorrow! The fact that my plans involve six boys and no other girls is . . . well . . . I know Mom wouldn't be happy about that. But seriously, Rick is the best and I think, with my experiences at the comic book shop, I've proven that I can be around guys and not end up pregnant. Sometimes I wonder if Mom actually knows how babies are made.

The kettle clicks just as I decide to keep my night's experiences vague.

"So let's see them," Mom says, holding out her hand.

"See what?" I ask.

"The photos you took. You're always snapping a million pictures whenever you go to one of these things. Let's see the action."

I put my hand over my jeans pocket. "Yeah, my um . . . phone . . . died. The battery crapped out. I'm going to charge it tonight and take a bunch of photos tomorrow. Besides, it's a three day thing, so no big deal right? Anyway, it got dark early so . . . um . . . not much to see . . . yeah."

I stop, realizing I'm talking way too much.

"That's too bad," she says. "Hopefully you'll get some shots tomorrow. Are you going to dress up for this or don't your superhero costumes fit in?"

"There were some superhero costumes there." I nod. "I just thought I would scout everything out today and dress up anime tomorrow. Want to see my outfit?"

"If it's one of those Japanese schoolgirl things, you aren't going," Mom says, crossing her arms.

I laugh. "Well, I guess it *is* a Japanese schoolgirl, but not the way you're thinking." I rush into my room and put on my Haruhi costume.

"Oh, you look darling!" she squeals as I come out, clapping her hands by her face like butterfly wings. "But why are you playing a boy?"

It takes an hour, over tea, to explain *Ouran High School*

Host Club to her, and anime in general. She eventually gets that I'm playing a girl who's playing a boy, though the plot of the show escapes her for the most part.

"But why her?" Mom asks. "I would have thought you would pick a girl with a big gun over a high school student."

"I guess I like the fact that Haruhi is straightforward. She's cheerful even though she lives the 'commoner's life' and she's not scared of a little hard work. She's practical, responsible, and isn't taken in by the charm of the hosts even though all the other girls are swooning. I also like how loyal she is to her friends, even when they drive her crazy with their stupid plans."

"So, this Haruhi," Mom says, "she's trying to improve herself by going to this school?"

"Yeah," I nod. "She wants to be a lawyer."

"That sounds great. I think I like her too. Maybe she'll inspire you to be a lawyer instead of a crime fighter." She winks, pushing herself to her feet and clearing our cups and the last crumbs of *lengua de gato*.

"Mom, I haven't wanted to be a crime fighter since I was six."

"Six?" Mom laughs.

"Okay, maybe twelve. But seriously!"

Mom continues to laugh. "Well, I'm glad you're happy. I'm going to head to bed. You have a good night."

I yawn. "I will. I'm just going to tell Tya how it went and hit the hay too."

Mom frowns. "Tya was there. Shouldn't she know how it went?"

Cold prickles shoot down my spine as I realize my blunder two seconds too late. I fight to turn the situation around. "I meant Cora. She's into anime and wanted to know about the convention. I must have Tya on the brain from spending the whole day with her." I laugh, standing up and quick-walking to my room, hoping my mom buys another of my lies.

I log onto Facebook and send Tya the pictures from my phone. A message from her pops up a second later.

Mariam! You look incredible! How did it go?

Everyone loved your costume. And that guy, Samir, from the comic book shop, was even there. And . . .

And . . .?

I got his phone number!

Tya sends me a dozen thumbs-up icons before asking, *Did you see a Tamaki?*

A warm flush shoots through my body. *Not only did I see him, I'm hanging out with him and the whole Ouran High School Host Club tomorrow!*

Oooh! Lucky! What's he like?

I think. *He's Asian. Maybe Korean or Chinese. I'm not sure. He doesn't really have an accent or anything.*

Is he hot?

He's Tamaki. What do you think? I type.

Tya sends back a smiley face before asking, *Is he charming?*

Charming doesn't even begin to describe him, I say.

Sounds like true love. She posts some hearts, then says, *I gotta go. Mom is mad I'm on my phone. It's just after midnight here and the party is still in full swing. Have fun tomorrow and tell me EVERYTHING!*

I send her a thumbs up and then log off, giving a yawn. I decide to actually contact Cora through Skype. Doing that will get rid of the lie and, besides, I did promise to tell her about Otafest.

When she answers, she waves the latest *Teen Titans* comic at the screen. "This better be important, Mariam!" she snaps. "Because Superboy is getting his butt handed to him."

"And what a butt it is," I reply.

"Oh, yes!" Cora laughs. "Hey, how did your thing go tonight? Did you actually wear the costume?"

"Yup." I tell her about all the photos I posed for and the people I met, including Rick.

"What's he like?" Cora asks, leaning into the camera.

"Well, I think he's a bit of a player, but he's charming."

"A player, huh? You have to watch those," Cora says, her eyes flashing. "Your mom okay with all this?"

"She, uh, doesn't know," I say.

"How'd you manage that?" Cora asks.

"You know . . ." I look away from the screen. Not wanting to explain.

"Lying," Cora finishes for me.

"Well," I frown. "It's her own fault. If she would just trust me more, I wouldn't have to do this."

"I don't see how lying to her is going to get her to trust you more."

"It was lie or not go to Otafest," I explain. "The choice was obvious."

"You couldn't have worked it out?" Cora asks.

"Why take the chance? You're just lucky you have Grandma Poitras around. She's way cooler than my mom." "If you say so," Cora says. "Hey, guess who I saw today?"

"Superboy," I joke.

She swoons. "I wish! But no, Rose and her mom dropped by today."

"Really? How is she?"

"Getting better, I think. They were here finalizing the sale of the house. We're meeting up tomorrow for a bit. Grandma Poitras is taking us to the Nerdvana. She wants to pick up the latest *Unbeatable Squirrel Girl* comic."

"I still think it's funny your Grandma is into that. Well, tell everyone I say hi."

"Will do." Cora signs off.

Closing my laptop, I picture tomorrow in my mind. Haruhi and Tamaki, hanging out, just like in the anime. Not to mention the twins, who are actually kind of cute. And Samir too. I'm exhausted, but I really don't know how I'm going to sleep. Tomorrow will be amazing times a million.

CHAPTER SIXTEEN

A TANGLE OF STUPID LIES

Peering in the mirror, I put in a final dab of gel just to keep everything in place. My tie is perfect — after sixteen tries. The purple stripe runs horizontally across the knot and vertically down the tie. I pull my baby blue sports jacket into place, smooth out the creases, and run my fingers over the embroidered Ouran Academy crest, my favourite part of the costume.

Tamaki better be ready for his newest host!

With a big grin, I wink at the mirror. I am Haruhi Fujioka. This time I feel much more confident. Not that anything bad happened yesterday. I guess the Cosplay ≠ Consent signs and the Otafest volunteers stationed everywhere really do keep everyone safe.

"Still adorable," Mom says, kissing me on the cheek as I enter the kitchen.

"Thanks," I put my lunch in my satchel then grab the last piece of toast from the plate. "Gotta go!" With toast dangling out of my mouth, I head for the door.

"Sit down if you're eating," Mom scolds.

"Sorry," I say, coming back and sinking into a chair to eat like a human being. "But I'm running late."

It's already nine-thirty and Rick wanted me to meet him at ten for the photo shoot. I don't think I'm going to make it in time. It takes almost an hour to get to the university from my place.

"I'll drive you, I don't have to be at work for an hour," Mom offers. "We can swing by and pick up Tya too."

The toast drops out of my hand. I scramble to pick it up.

"Umm . . . Tya's running even later," I say, the jumble of lies falling out of my mouth like living, squirming things. "Something to do with her brother, I think. She said she would meet me down there."

"Maybe you should wait for her," Mom says. "You know how I feel about you going on your own."

My brain heats up, trying to find a way through this maze I've built for myself. I lift my chin and smile. "I won't be alone," I say.

"You won't? Who else will be there?" Mom scowls. She's getting suspicious. Not good.

"I met some friends yesterday. Actually, I know them from school. I'll be hanging out with them until Tya arrives. Besides, everyone at Otafest is wonderful." I try to look relaxed even though my hands shake in my lap and my mouth has gone as dry as the toast.

"Fine, if you have other friends there, let's go," Mom says. "But I want to meet them."

I wonder if Samir and Jemma would show up at the parking lot to save my butt if I called. Probably not. I mean, I've only met Jemma twice and not for very long each time and Samir is a boy. It's the same reason I can't call Rick and his friends. Mom would flip if she knew I was only hanging out with guys this morning. I chuck my toast in the garbage, not

103

hungry anymore, and Mom and I head out the door.

It's not until we're almost at Otafest that I realize there's a bigger problem. Mom has had very little exposure to cosplay and some of the costumes are a bit on what she might consider the racy side. Silently I pray that everyone near the parking lot is fully clothed, while keeping my eyes open for costumes that might offend her, my nerves pouring molten lava into my belly.

"What is that?" Mom asks, pulling in. She's pointing at two kids dressed up in Pikachu and Charmander onesies.

"Pokémon characters. Funny, huh?" I laugh uneasily.

"Look at that!" Mom says. She gazes at a guy in an Assassin's Creed outfit, loads of belts crisscrossing and his face nearly covered. "Are you sure this place is safe?"

"He's just acting out a character from a video game. He's probably a nice guy." I spot a girl in a fabulous dress full of bows, lace, and pink satin. I point it out to my mom, hoping to take her mind off the assassin. "Look, there's a princess." Then I realize it's a boy. Crap.

Luckily Mom seems oblivious. "She's pretty. So, where are your friends?"

"Oh, I was going to text them when I . . ." as I make up yet another excuse, I spot two people walking down the sidewalk. One of them is America from *Hetalia*. The other is dressed as Colonel Mustang from *Fullmetal Alchemist*. Could it be? I squint through the glaring sunlight. It is! "Samir! Jemma!" I wave my arm. They look in my direction and come over.

"Mariam!" Samir smiles.

"This is my mom," I say, introducing everyone. "Did you guys just get here?" I ask, acting like we were planning to meet up in the parking lot all along.

"Yeah," Samir says. "We're going to do a bit of shopping before things get too busy. Then we're going to the *Hetalia*: Ask a Nation panel. After all, I thought I would fit in." He pulls his best America stance.

"And then I'm going to enter the Crossplay Pageant," Jemma says.

"That sounds like fun. You'll win for sure!" I cheer.

"Thanks," Jemma replies. "That's a great Haruhi costume. Just about as good as the one you were wearing yesterday. Though that one might have been more detailed."

"What one from yesterday?" Mom asks. "I thought you didn't dress up."

I look at Jemma and she looks at me. The panic I'm feeling shoots right through my eyes into hers. Jemma scrambles to reply. "Oh, it was just a coat from her friend, what was her name again?"

"Tya," I say, also scrambling. "Yeah, Tya lent me her coat from one of the animes we watch together. That's not really dressing up. Anyway, Mom," I say, gesturing towards the car, "I'm good now. Found my friends. Ready to get started. I'm sure Tya will be here soon. You know, when she's done with her brother and stuff."

"You don't need to be embarrassed by me, you know," Mom says, looking hurt.

"I know," I say, my teeth playing over my lip. "It's just . . ." I wish I could introduce Mom to this world. But she's so over-protective lately, neither of us would have any fun. Besides, with her around I can't meet up with Rick and the Host Club, or hang out with Samir by himself, and that would ruin everything. "Can I go now, Mom?" I ask, looking away.

Mom frowns. "Fine. Be safe. Call me when you're done and

I'll come and get you." She turns and gets back into the car.

Samir waves. "It was nice meeting you," he calls.

As she drives away, Jemma asks, "So, your mom doesn't know about yesterday's outfit?"

"Not exactly." I shrug. "She would never approve."

"Sorry if I ratted you out."

"It's fine," I say. My phone starts ringing. "Hi."

"Haruhi, where are you?" the voice demands. "We've been waiting seven minutes and I can't go on much longer."

"Oh, sorry, Rick. Uh . . . I mean, Tamaki," I say, remembering how he wants to be called after his character this weekend. "I'll be there right away. My mom just dropped me off."

"Hurry, princess. Please." He hangs up.

I put my phone back into my costume's satchel. "Gotta run."

"Can't you hang out with us?" Samir asks, his voice so sweet I want to wrap myself in it.

"I promised this group of Ouran cosplayers I'd do a photo shoot and hang out with them for a bit," I apologise. "Maybe I can catch up with you guys at the *Hetalia* thing. I actually wanted to see that."

"Great! Hopefully we'll see you there. Call me if you want to meet up somewhere else too, okay?" Samir says.

"Okay," I smile, warmth pouring into me. I've never had any boys wanting my attention, and now there are two of them. I can't help the hugely stupid grin that pulls on my face as I hurry down the path toward the hill. I will definitely be seeing Samir later. Right after Rick. Why can't Otafest be forever?

★★★ CHAPTER SEVENTEEN

SO MUCH ATTENTION

I spot all the boys from *Ouran High School Host Club* at the base of the hill in their identical school uniforms. My inner fangirl does a little squeal of joy. So cool! Rick scans the crowd twirling a rose between his fingers. His blond hair blows in the breeze. My heart flutters. He really does look like Tamaki. Tobias, playing studious Kyoya, reads over the schedule and Lee, his little brother as I found out yesterday, kicks his toe in the dirt while holding his stuffed rabbit upside-down by the leg. The twins, Sung and Hyun, play rock, paper, scissors — always landing on the same thing, much to Paul's delight. Paul, who is playing the silent Mori, still looks more than a little intimidating. Though when he laughs, he seems much friendlier.

"Sorry I'm late," I say, a little out of breath.

"You're not very late," the twins say in unison, then crack up.

"Sorry," Sung says, "that happens sometimes."

"Yeah," Hyun smiles. "We spend too much time together."

Rick's attention snaps over to me, a smile spreading across his face. His eyes shimmer as he takes me in. "You're perfect," he gasps. Then, recovering his composure and pulling himself to his full height, he announces, "Let me introduce our newest host, Haruhi."

I bow, following the script. "I am happy to serve you."

Without warning, Rick rushes over, grabs me in his arms, and spins me around in a tight embrace, making me dizzy and crushed. He gushes, "You're so cute! You're good! Amazingly good! Oh, you're so cute!"

I realize that Rick is acting out a scene from the first episode of *Ouran High School Host Club.* Luckily I know the line that will get this to stop. "Mori *Senpai,* help me!"

Mori, or rather Paul, comes over and does exactly what the Mori in the anime does. He picks me up by my armpits and holds me in the air, before setting me on the ground once more, a half-smile playing across his face.

"Thanks," I breathe, wobbling from dizziness. Rick really takes cosplaying seriously.

"Men!" Rick calls out, bringing the attention back on himself. "It is our responsibility as members of the elite Ouran Host Club, to make every girl happy. To do this we are going to take photos. Let's go."

We march over to a smaller hill where a girl has camera set up on a tripod, along with some lights and diffusers. Rick gets us in position and directs our various poses, most of which are from either the anime or the manga and involve blowing rose petals or other props. He does some individual photos too. It's really fun. I feel like I'm part of a theatre group. Other Otafest-goers stand around and watch. When we're done they give a round of applause. Rick throws what's left of the rose petals at them and blows kisses. Then we pose for fan photographs.

It's been a good hour by the time we wrap it up. I look at the schedule. *Hetalia:* Ask a Nation is about to start and I'm still not completely sure where all the rooms are so I figure I better get a move on. "Well, Rick, thanks for the fun but I have to go."

"Call me Tamaki while we're here," he croons.

"Sorry, Tamaki," I repeat. "Anyway, thanks again. I'm going to see a panel now."

"Which one?" asks Tobias.

"*Hetalia*," I say. "Want to come?"

Tobias smiles, and it looks like he's going to say yes when Rick catches his attention with a subtle shake of his head. "What do you think, *Senpai*?" Tobias, asks instead.

Rick bows his head, fingers pinching the bridge of his nose. "I am your King. And as your King I think it is best if we went to Japanese Tea Tasting. That is more befitting the Host Club than vulgar politics."

"I don't care about tea tasting," I say. And Samir isn't going to be there. "I'll just catch up with you guys later, okay?"

"I don't want to go either," Lee chimes in. "I brought my 3DS so I can trade Pokémon in the Pokémon League room." He scowls at Tobias. "You promised."

"*Senpai*?" Tobias says again, ignoring his brother. "A panel would be fun. And Haruhi is going."

Although it's kind of cool being known as my character, it's weird being called by something other than my name. "Uh . . . it's Mariam. Okay?" I say.

An awkward silence fills the space. Tobias shuffles his feet. Sung, Hyun, and Paul look everywhere but at Rick or me.

"Well," I finally say, trying to set things right again. "How about we each go to whatever we want right now then meet up afterwards?"

Tobias smiles. "That sounds like a great . . ." His words trail off as Rick's eyes narrow.

"Now how would it look if we split up?" Rick asks with a sweep of his arm. "People come to these events to see their favourite characters. To see anime in real life. If we wander off alone, we will be disappointing people and . . ." He lets loose a seductive smile, taking my hand in his, lips brushing my cheek. "You'll be disappointing me."

My chest tingles with butterflies, but I can't tell if it's excitement or anxiety.

"But . . ." I start to say, however Rick/Tamaki has already turned his attention on Lee and is scolding him for wanting to leave and reminding him who bought his Otafest ticket.

Lee turns away, face red, teeth gritted.

Tobias tells Lee to stop being so irritating and just do as he's told. Then he goes over to stand beside Rick. "Okay, *Senpai*, tea tasting it is," he announces.

"Sounds like a blast," Sung says, not really sounding that convinced.

Hyun shrugs and Paul grunts. Lee looks at me, waiting to see if I'm going to fall in line too. I'm sure his mom told him to stick with his big brother and with Tobias being so loyal, Lee is trapped.

I feel bad. At least I can leave whenever I want.

"You going?" Lee sulks.

"Yes, Haruhi, are you going to disappoint our clients?" Rick asks.

I frown. "I don't usually think of the general public as my clients." I'm starting to see why Haruhi is generally so annoyed by Tamaki.

"But they want to see you. They want to see . . . us." Rick winks. "Together."

"Come on," Tobias says, in a low voice, "just do it."

I shrug. I only started watching *Hetalia* recently, so I'm not a mega-fan. And I'll see Samir later at the crossplay contest, so . . . "Fine," I sigh, shoving my own interests aside for the greater good. "Let's go to tea tasting. I'm sure it will be fun."

"All right!" Rick says, spreading his arms. "Our little family will never be apart." He pats Lee on the head then takes off at a quick pace expecting everyone to follow.

"Jerk," Lee mutters under his breath. Then, balancing the rabbit over his shoulder, he pulls out his 3DS and plays as he walks.

★★★

After the tea tasting, which was actually way more interesting than I thought it was going to be, Rick directs us to the Maid Café, where he has booked us a table. He buys me tea and cake, and treats me like royalty, calling me princess constantly and even going so far as to stir my tea and feed me, until I snatch the fork away. Then he asks if I'll feed him.

"Uh, why?" I ask.

"I can be your client," Rick says.

"But you're a boy," I say, using Ouran logic. "As Haruhi I can only entertain girls."

"Not if I were gay," Rick says.

"You're not," I reply.

"What if you were practicing?" Rick smiles. "Come on. Let's see your host moves."

"Fine. How's this?" I pick up the fork and stab it into his cake before pointing it rather aggressively at his mouth. Then I think of the perfect Haruhi quote to go with this situation. "You know, *Senpai*, this could be considered sexual harassment."

Rick looks shocked. "You don't need to be like that."

I laugh but no one else does. Crap. I try another line Haruhi uses whenever Tamaki is upset. "Come on, *Senpai*, would you please stop growing mushrooms in other people's closets?"

Rick forces a smile. "You don't need to say that. I'm not sulking. I just thought feeding me cake would be fun for you."

I bite my lip. "Sorry. I didn't mean to hurt your feelings."

Rick claps his hands. "No harm done!" Then he shoots Tobias a hard look. "What did I plan next?"

Tobias looks at his notepad. "We're going to the *Ouran High School Host Club* panel."

I open my own schedule and spot the contest Jemma was entering. It's up next. "Sorry, I can't join you. There's the cross-play pageant I have to go to."

"But you're not in crossplay," Paul says. "You're a girl playing a boy that's playing a girl. I mean . . . what? Wait. That's not right."

"You're hurting my head," the twins say together. They look at each other and scowl. "Stop doing that," they say again in unison. "I mean it," they continue. "Ahh, forget it," they finish.

Paul, Tobias, and I crack up.

Rick wraps his arms around his body and looks away. "Leave us if you must," he says. "We can go on our own. Incomplete. To an *Ouran High School Host Club* panel. Looking . . ." he sends a sigh towards the ceiling, "ridiculous."

"You didn't have a Haruhi before I met you," I say, a scowl starting to form. "What difference would it make?"

"But people have seen you with us now. We're the only complete set here. Well," he clasps his hands. "We were."

"So we have to do everything together?" I ask.

"Well, yes," Tobias says. "You and Tamaki *Senpai* are love interests so you kind of have to be with each other."

"But Haruhi doesn't love Tamaki," I challenge. "Well, not at the beginning."

Rick takes my chin in the palm of his hand, sending an electric jolt through me. "Allow me to win you over."

I blush. Words scramble in my head. His smile is so seductive. So perfect. Haruhi wouldn't leave him if he needed her. I guess I shouldn't either. "Okay, fine, let's go," I say, sending my thoughts to Jemma at the crossplay pageant and wishing her luck in my absence. I would have liked to see her but at least I am in the right costume for this panel and Rick is right. I should be at his side for this.

CHAPTER EIGHTEEN

HE LIKES YOU

Finally the panel lets out. My stomach growls.

"I'm bored and hungry," Lee complains.

Rick decides we should go for sushi. I bow out of that. I don't have any extra money for take-out. Instead I offer to find us a table. Lee takes off, yelling something about a burger and having his own money, before Tobias can say anything.

At the table I look at myself in the mirrored ceiling and sigh. I'm usually not so easily pushed around, but somehow Rick has a hold on me. Every time I try to leave and do something on my own, he acts hurt and upset, like I've wounded his ego, and I'm drawn back in. Then again, it is kind of nice having him fawn over me. I've never been called princess so much in my life. I wonder if he really likes me, or just the character I'm playing.

I wonder if it matters.

Lee is the first one back. He sits next to me and unwraps his burger, taking a big bite. "You should be careful around Rick," he says, chewing.

"Why?" I ask. "He's kind of bossy, but that's not anything

to be afraid of. You could stand up to him, you know. I'd have your back."

Lee shakes his head. "That's not what I meant." He focuses on his drink, looking nervous.

"What did you mean, then?" I ask.

"Don't say anything, but two years ago, before Rick got into all this anime crap, he might have done something to a girl."

"Might have done what?"

"I don't know exactly, but there were rumours."

"What kind of rumours?" I ask, suspicious.

"Rick and my brother both liked this girl in their drama club. They were all in a play together. She was Juliet, and Rick was Romeo, but Tobias was the one who actually asked her out. When Rick found out, he got really mad. He told Tobias to break up with her. He thought because she was his girlfriend on stage, she was his in real life too."

"So what did Tobias do?" I ask.

Lee shrugs, "Break up with her."

"Well that was stupid."

"I guess, but what Rick did was worse," Lee says.

"What'd he do?"

"He went over to the girl's house and attacked her."

"Attacked her?" I ask. "Are you sure?"

"People said he forced her to do things. Bad things. Like, really bad," Lee says, glancing in the direction of the sushi shop where the guys have reached the front of the line.

"Do you think it's true?" I ask, a knot of uncertainty forming in my gut.

Lee shrugs. "Rick said he only talked to her. Tobias said that too. But the rumours were around."

"What did the girl say?" I ask.

"Nothing. She wouldn't talk about it. But she did quit the play two days before it was supposed to go on."

Not sure if I buy what Lee is selling, I ask, "If Rick is so horrible, why does Tobias hang out with him?"

"Tobias and Rick have been friends ever since grade one. Rick's always in charge and Tobias is always his, I don't know, sidekick. It's just the way things are. Anyway," Lee lowers his voice as the guys head over, "don't tell anyone I told you, okay? I don't need Rick freaking out on me."

"I've decided," Rick says, sitting down across from me and opening his container of California rolls, "you are coming with me to the dance tonight. We can gaze into each other's souls while the lights shimmer off your beautiful eyes. You'll be the loveliest petal floating on the dance floor," Rick sings.

"Well, you have a lot of faith," I laugh.

Rick looks enthusiastic, not dangerous. I wonder if Lee is telling the truth. He *has* been pretty mad at Rick all day and it's obvious he doesn't want to be here. Maybe he's getting back at Rick with made-up story. I mean, the thought of Rick doing anything to one of his precious princesses seems pretty farfetched, especially since there was a play at stake. He really likes the whole acting thing.

"So will you dance with me?" Rick asks, holding out his hand, violet eyes sparkling.

"Yeah, will you come?" Hyun asks. "It would be nice to actually have a girl with us for a change."

I shrug. The dance would be fun. And it's not like I'd be alone with Rick, so even if he did try to pull whatever Lee is claiming, I'd be safe. Besides, maybe Samir will be there. Wow, two totally hot guys at the same dance. A blush overtakes my face. I dip my head, hoping the guys don't notice. "I have to ask my mom first."

I pull out my cell phone and dial. Mom answers on the second ring, the sounds of the diner behind her. "Mom?" I ask. "Could I could stay a bit late? There's a dance I just found out about."

"Is Tya going?" Mom asks.

If Tya were here, I'm sure she would be going. How could she not? It would be the perfect place to show off her costume. "Yeah," I lie.

"Is her mom picking her up after?"

"Uh . . . we were just going to take the C-Train back."

Mom clucks her tongue. "I don't know. It doesn't sound safe."

"I can look after myself," I snap. "I might be a girl, but I'm not helpless."

Mom lets out a long sigh. "Mariam."

"Mom, seriously. I'm fine."

There's a pause. I listen to the clatter of dishes and muffled conversation in the background. Finally she says, "I guess you can go to the dance. But call me when you're done and I'll come and get you."

"Okay, Mom, thanks!" Now my only problem is figuring out a reason Tya won't be coming home with me.

★★★

After a full afternoon of being glued to Rick's side, I'm just about done. My head pounds and I'm exhausted. He insists we accept every request for a picture, even the ones that have me in awkward positions or kissing other girls. It's too much. But every time I protest, Rick reminds me, with a tap of his finger on my Ouran crest, of the unspoken contract that comes with wearing the Host Club uniform.

I'm starting to miss being Black Rock Shooter.

We head up the stairs to the dance. Rick grips my arm like I'm going to run away which, after we pass the through the doors, feels like a good idea. The room is just a bit smaller than my school gym and packed. Lights bounce off the walls and illuminate metal armor and sparkly wings. The air is bursting with sweat, hormones, and the distinct odor of melting grease paint. I get grey makeup on my jacket as soon as I enter.

Rick squeezes my elbow more tightly and wraps his arm around me, accidently brushing my breast. "It's okay," he says. "You're safe."

Alarm bells go off. Lee's story punches to the forefront of my mind. I pull back and take some personal space. "I'm fine," I say. "You don't need to glom onto me."

Rick looks hurt. "But I'm protecting you from these ruffians."

"I can protect myself."

"I don't want their dirty hands all over you. After all, you're mine," he responds.

"I'm not anyone's," I growl, getting more and more irritated, "and you have *your* dirty hands all over me."

Rick laughs. "But I'm supposed to have my hands all over you." He winks.

I turn my back on him and check out the room. The music pulses. It's loud enough to make my ears ring and my heart change beat. People in wigs and rapidly decaying cosplay dance and mingle. A screen flashes anime clips while lights cast multicoloured shadows on the walls. It's exhausting just trying to stand up. I look through the mash of bouncing bodies to see if I can find Samir, but I can't make him out. Maybe he didn't come to this. Maybe this isn't his thing.

It might not be mine either.

Rick has his hands on me again, this time tight on my shoulders, his chest pressing on the back of my neck. "This is going to be fun, don't you think?" His rose bobs in my face. I squirm out of his grip again. "Oh, come on. Stop playing hard to get," Rick whines.

"Stop grabbing me," I retort.

I move between Sung and Hyun. The twins ask me to dance at the same time, then laugh at themselves. I laugh too, more out of relief that these two are at least normal. Sung takes my hand and leads me out to the dance floor. I'm sweating to death in my sports jacket and thankful I don't have to wear a wig for my Haruhi costume. I don't know how some of these other cosplayers are doing it. The song ends and Hyun takes his brother's place for one of my favourite anime theme songs. I forget my shyness and let loose. Hyun goes crazy too and within a few minutes we're both laughing our heads off at how ridiculous we look.

When I get back, I join Tobias and Lee by the wall. Lee has his 3DS out and is ignoring everyone in the room. The Pokémon theme song starts up. I grab him and drag him somewhat unwillingly onto the dance floor. I know he's mainly here as a prop, so I want him to have some fun. After a few awkward moments he gets into it in a big way, singing along at the top of his lungs and pumping his fist in the air. He can't help himself — he is a true Pokémon fan. By the end Lee has a big grin on his face and a story to tell. He actually danced with a high school girl. That's got to give him some cred — even for a nerd.

I ask Tobias if he wants to dance. Well, mostly I yell, the music is pretty deafening. He looks over at Rick. Rick looks back with a smile, but even I catch the slight shake of his head and the glare he slips the twins. Sung and Hyun, oblivious to Rick's mood, scout out some girls, talking in unison again.

Tobias, steps back. "I better not," he says.

"It's a free world," I counter.

"Yeah but . . ." He looks away. "It's just not a good idea."

I look at Lee and wonder if I'm going to get him in trouble, but I have to know. "Did Rick do something to your girlfriend?"

"What?" Tobias asks, confused.

"When you were in the drama club together, did Rick do something to your girlfriend?"

Tobias scowls, fists automatically clenching. "Who told you that?"

I shrug.

"No," he answers.

"But she quit the play," I say. "Why?"

Tobias stiffens. "I've already told everyone, I don't know! Besides, that was two years ago, before Rick was into . . ." He looks around. "Anyway, it's over now. He's a different person."

"But did he —" I start.

"Can we talk about something else?" Tobias interrupts, trying to look bored.

"Fine," I smile, switching to a different tactic. "Dance with me."

"Forget it."

"Why?" I press.

"Because you're being a pest," Tobias snaps.

"Is it because you're scared of Rick?"

Tobias glares. "He's my best friend. Why would I be scared

of him? I'm not going dance with you because he likes you."

"Can he like me without grabbing at me?" I ask loud enough for Rick to hear, I hope.

"You're being too sensitive," Tobias says.

"I'm being too sensitive?" I rant. "Seriously?"

Tobias rolls his eyes. "I should get Lee home. Just do what Rick wants, okay?" He asks Rick if they're allowed to leave. It's sickening.

I turn to Paul ask if he wants to dance. "You should dance with Rick," he advises.

"I don't want to."

"You should still do it."

"Why?" I cross my arms.

"Because everyone expects it. You're Haruhi," Paul says.

"There's more to life than playing a character." I scowl.

"Maybe to you," Paul says, his eyes darting to Rick. "Listen, it's not that big a deal. Go make him happy."

"Not on your life." I head into the crowd. I'd like to find out if Samir is here. If he is, I'll dance with him — all night long, right in front of Rick. I'd like to see Rick try to manipulate Samir the way he manipulates everyone else.

★★★ CHAPTER NINETEEN

I'M NOT A PROSTITUTE

I push through the press of bodies, looking at every face. "Samir, where are you?"

Rick yells behind me. "Haruhi, come back!"

I keep walking, pulling out my phone to text Samir. Some guys in barbarian costumes block my way as they chat up two magical girl princesses. I type my message, thumbs flicking. *Are you at the dance?*

Rick catches up and locks onto my arm. "Where are you going?" he screams over the music.

"To look for my friend," I yell, shaking him loose.

"What friend? You don't know anyone here."

"I do too," I frown.

My phone chirps and vibrates. I glance at the text. He's replied with, *Yes. Are you?*

The barbarians shift, leaving a gap. I move forward, trying to get away while typing in my reply. *Yeah. I need a hero. Is America available?*

I hit send just as Rick grabs me again, a scowl twisting his practiced Tamaki look.

"You're lying," he says.

"I'm not! I have friends here!"

"Then where are they?"

I look hard, trying to catch sight of a bomber jacket and a star. I should have asked Samir specifically where he was.

"I'm waiting," Rick says, fingers pressing into my bicep.

Then I see him, half a room away. "Samir!" I pull away and wave over the heads of all the people in front of me. He doesn't see me. I wave again, but he's too busy looking at his phone to notice.

"That guy?" Rick shrugs. "He doesn't look like he knows you."

"He just doesn't see me." I wave harder. Jemma is beside him, but she's talking to a pirate girl and not paying attention. My stomach tenses. "Come on," I mutter to myself.

"Ha! If I was going to pick a fake friend," Rick snorts, "I'd pick someone who didn't look like such an idiot."

"Shut up!" I try to walk away, but it's really crowded. My phone vibrates again. Samir has texted, *I don't think America is the type of hero you need, but I can help. Where are you?*

I start to type but Rick snatches my phone away, holding it behind his back. He smiles, his eyes crinkling. "Aww, come on, princess." He leans into my ear, breath hot on my neck. "Don't be mad. I'm only having fun." A slow song starts playing. Rick grabs my hands and cocks his head to the side. "Dance with me."

"Give me back my phone," I say, losing sight of Samir as the crowd shifts.

"After our dance."

"I don't want to."

"But we must," he says.

"Stop telling me what to do!" I fume. "You've been doing

that all day. Pose for this person. Kiss that girl. Feed me cake. I've had enough!"

His lips twist, and his smile falters. "But I just . . ."

"Give it back!"

I push Rick in the chest with both my hands, making him drop the phone. As I go to grab it he yanks me onto the dance floor, his arms wrapping me tight to his chest, hips swaying. "One dance, then you can have anything you want." His bulging crotch moves in slow circles against me. "You make me so hot, Haruhi. I want to be with you now." His breath trembles in my ear. "Right now."

I fight to get away, but he's strong and I can't do anything.

"Calm down," he croons. "You know the story. We end up together. We get married and have kids. It says so in the manga."

My heart pounds. Everything slows down. I try to remember what Grandma Poitras taught me. Focus on relaxing.

"That's my girl," he mutters, thinking I'm giving in.

With him off guard, I slide my arms into the small gap that's formed between our bodies and push. He falls back, flapping into the other dancers. Before he can get back up, I speed away, ignoring my phone still lost on the floor, ignoring the other dancers, ignoring the Otafest volunteers. My skin crawls from his touch. My stomach heaves. I have to get away. Zigzagging through the sweat-slick crowd, I tug open the glass doors. My feet pound the stairs, pulse fluttering, breath burning. Behind me the clunk of doors opening again sounds.

Rick.

I race to the bottom of the staircase, shoes echoing in the empty hall and flee past the double doors into the cool night air. There's a grunt as Rick yanks the outer door too, trying to catch up. I turn left and run down the narrow sidewalk dodging toward a group of trees, my lungs huffing in time with my feet. I plan to lose him on the campus, but as I run I realize two things. I don't know my way around and now I'm alone.

Grandma Poitras warned me about this. I should have stayed at the dance. I've played right into his hands.

My legs quiver as I realize how bad things are, tears blur my vision, and hiccupped sobs cut my breathing. I look for help, but no one is around. Rick's feet pound right behind me. A dark clutch of trees appears on my right. I dart towards them, aiming to hide. Rick catches the strap of my satchel, yanking me to a halt.

"What is your problem?" he growls. His gentle Tamaki face is gone. Instead it's replaced with frustration, his eyes bloodshot from too many hours in his violet contacts, his lips lifted in a snarl.

"Let me go!" I shout, trying to dodge past him.

His fingers crush my shoulder, pushing me into the trunk of a birch tree, his other hand clamps onto my wrist. "You promised me a dance."

"I changed my mind," I say, throwing a knee at him and missing. This seemed so straightforward in practice.

He squeezes harder. "So you'll dance with everyone else, but not me!"

"Everyone else was nice to me."

"I was nice to you all day! I treated you like royalty!" He bows his head and mutters. "I thought *otakus* were different. I thought you understood! But you're just like everyone else!"

"Understood what?" I look around for help, but the paths are deserted and trail off into the darkness.

"How to make it real."

"That's not how cosplay works," I growl.

"That's exactly how it works!" Rick shouts. "Why else would you dress up?"

"Because I like Haruhi. She's an awesome character."

Rick snorts, his grip not letting up. "Liar. You don't *like* her. You want to *be* her."

"That's insane," I say.

Rick chuckles and shakes his head. "Don't deny the truth. You want nothing to do with the real world."

I open my mouth to protest, but Rick is right. Like Samir said, the real world is hard. Sometimes it's easier to be someone else.

Rick continues. "Haruhi is in love with Tamaki. So if you play her you have to love me."

"But I didn't dress up for you. I dressed up for me. And no matter how much I want it to be real, it's still just pretend."

"Is it?" Rick smirks. "You played along didn't you?"

"That doesn't mean —"

"You were my Haruhi and I was your Tamaki."

"That's not —" I protest.

"And, so long as you were getting what you wanted, we could be real." Rick brings his face in close, his voice a harsh whisper. "I got your photograph taken, bought you tea and cake, spent money on you."

"I never asked —"

"And as soon as *I* want something, you say 'no. It's pretend. Leave me alone.'" Rick releases my wrist and pushes his sweat-soaked hair from his face. "But it's like any host club tab: eventually you have to pay up."

A twang of guilt vibrates through me. I mean, I was all for being Haruhi and pretending he was Tamaki. He did buy me cake at the Maid Café. And that photographer must have cost a fortune. I have to admit, I did play along. It was fun living the fantasy. And now that he wants something from me, I change my mind. Maybe I do owe him.

But then I remember the panels I missed, the poses I had to do even after I said no, his crotch hard against me, and my guilt evaporates. Instead I yell, "I am not a prostitute! Just because you bought me things, or spent time with me, it doesn't mean I owe you anything! And you aren't part of a real host club. There is no tab!"

Rick slams his hand against the tree trunk, right by my head, making me flinch. "It's always the same with girls like you. I give and you take, take, take. You wanted to be Haruhi. Now follow the damn script and fall in love with me!"

My body trembles, adrenaline lighting up every nerve-ending. "There is no script! Why does everyone else in this whole place know that except you?" I try to push past him but he grabs my wrist again. "Let me leave!" I demand.

"No! We're seeing this through. You are Haruhi. I am Tamaki. We're going to be together, right now."

I shake my head, words falling out in a rush. "No! I'm Mariam. You're Rick. I get to choose who I'm with. Not some anime. Not some crazy fantasy."

He stops, pulls himself upright, anger pouring off of him in near-visible waves. "I told you not to call me Rick!"

He yanks me tight to his hardening groin, his cheek brushing my ear. "You know you want me," he hisses. "Don't deny it."

"Stop," I plead, my voice a desperate whisper. "Please."

I don't want to end up like Rose.

"Mariam!" My name is faint on the night air. "Mariam, where are you?"

Rick stiffens. His crotch softens. Still, he doesn't let go. Instead he leans down, crushing his lips against mine, tongue sweeping the front of my clenched teeth. Then he growls, "One kiss and one dance. That's all I ever wanted. And remember . . ." He reaches out, fingers clamping onto my chest and pulling away with the sound of ripping stiches and shredding fabric. "You brought this on yourself."

Then Rick jogs off into the darkness. I collapse on the grass, fingers clutching my torn blazer, hiccupped sobs shaking my body.

★★★ CHAPTER TWENTY

I'M SUCH AN IDIOT

I can't stop the tears from coming. The patch Tya made for me is gone. The jacket is ripped and stitches hang loose.

"Mariam!"

I hear people shouting out my name. I try to call back but my throat is locked up. Luckily the twins spot me.

"She's here," they say, running over, followed by Paul, Samir, and Jemma.

"Mariam, what happened?" Samir asks.

I cover my face, sobs still coming on hard. He goes to take my arm but I pull away, still shaking all over.

"Rick . . ." I start to say.

"Rick hurt you?" Sung and Hyun say in unison, only it isn't funny. They look as shocked as I feel.

Paul shakes his head. "But he's — he's not like that, is he? Unless . . ."

"What?" Jemma demands. "Tsk. Never mind! I'm calling security." She walks away, dialing the number.

Paul explains. "There were rumours, a couple years back. Something about a girl Tobias liked. People said Rick might have done something to her, but no charges were ever laid."

Samir scowls. "If there were rumours, why did you let Mariam leave with him?"

"I didn't let anyone do anything!" Paul says, frustrated. "I came with you to find her didn't I?"

"Where is Rick?" Sung asks.

"I — I don't know. He ran off." I point.

"We'll find him," Paul says, dashing into the darkness with Hyun and Sung following.

Samir sits down beside me on the grass, silent. Even with his costume he's still himself. Kind, gentle, and respectful, all the things a guy should be. I shake my head, leaning my forehead on my knees. "I'm such an idiot," I say. "Rick treated me so nice but then he — he . . ." I feel his crotch pressed against me, his lips crushing mine, his breath hissing, *"You brought this on yourself."* I fight for air.

"It's okay," Samir says.

"It's not. He wanted this," I motion to my ruined outfit, "to be real." I look up. "And I wanted it too for a while."

Samir tips his head to the stars, fingers interlaced on his knees. "I think we all do, in a way. It's easier to pretend to be someone else. It's scripted. We know what to expect. But we also know it's not real. That this," he waves his hand over his costume, "is just a reality vacation. I guess that's what makes it fun." Samir looks at me, "Rick exploited that to get what he wanted. Or tried to."

I nod. "Yeah. He seemed to be working really hard to keep everyone's fantasy under his control."

"It sounds like he has the problem," Samir says. "Not you."

"Still," I sigh, "I should have seen it earlier and left."

"If you did, he would have replaced you with someone else. Rick needs help. He's probably done this a few times."

I pull off my baby blue sports jacket and tug at the hanging thread. "I don't think I ever want to cosplay again."

"I understand," Samir says, "but remember, it wasn't how you were dressed that caused this. It was Rick. So don't blame yourself or your costume. It's not your fault."

"Thanks." I smile. Then a thought occurs to me. "How did you know to look for me?"

"I saw you push Rick. I figured something was up, but by the time I made it across the room, you were gone." He reaches into his pocket. "Then I found this."

I take my phone from his hand.

"How did you know it was mine?" I ask.

Samir chuckles. "No one else has a phone older than mine."

I make a note to myself to thank Mom for her hand me downs. "But how did you end up with Hyun, Sung, and Paul?" I ask.

"When Jemma and I went outside I heard them calling your name. I guess they were worried too. We teamed up to find you."

"Security is on their way." Jemma says, coming back. "They'll be here in a minute."

"But . . ." I protest. "What if —"

"Just be honest and things will work out," Jemma says, pulling off her black wig and wiping at her forehead. "They need to know about Rick before he hurts someone else."

Nerves fluttering, I try to think of Batgirl. She would want justice. She would turn this scumbag in. But with my wrist aching and body trembling, I don't feel like a superhero. I don't even feel like pretending to be one. The whole thing seems hollow and fake.

A big security guy with a kind face, who introduces himself as Mark, leads us to an empty room. He gets me a blanket to help with my shivering and starts filling out a form. He asks my age, phone number, and address. He also asks for my mom's name and cell phone number. I give him Rick's description, phone number, and picture, then go over the events. I explain everything that happened, glancing at Samir and Jemma for courage. When I get to the part where Rick attacked me, I can't stop shaking. But Mark lets me take my time and, when I'm done, he says he's glad I came forward. Then he excuses himself from the room.

"Thanks for helping me," I say to Samir and Jemma. I'm feeling a bit stronger. Talking about it is like shedding a toxic layer.

Mark comes back into the room, his face neutral. "Okay, here's what's going to happen. What Rick did is considered sexual assault, which means the police and your mom have been called."

My stomach drops. My blood freezes. "But . . . all he did was kiss me."

"Any unwanted touching is considered sexual assault. It's a crime."

I cover my mouth, trying to keep it together. "I can't tell my . . ."

"It's going to be okay," Mark says, misunderstanding my fear. "The police are sending over a female officer who's really good with this kind of stuff. She'll get the report started."

I nod, shaking. My mom. She'll know I lied.

Oh god.

Samir comes and sits beside me. Mark takes his and Jemma's statements while we wait. The white clock with its large black numbers ticks down the minutes.

As afraid as I am, when Mom arrives, I fall sobbing into her arms. Mark excuses himself to get the report ready for the police. Samir and Jemma also go outside to wait, giving us some privacy.

"Mariam! Are you all right? Where's Tya?" Mom asks, pulling me tight in a protective hug.

My stomach drops again. Tya. I forgot. I was supposed to be with Tya. "She left," I say.

"Left? When?" Mom pulls back and looks at me hard, her gaze critical.

I shrug. "A while ago. Before the dance."

Mom scowls. "You said you were going to the dance with Tya. What's going on?"

"Her mom said she couldn't stay but . . ." I scramble for an explanation. "Jemma and Samir were going to the dance too so I figured it would be all right."

Mom doesn't look satisfied. "If the situation changed, you should have called. You being there without Tya wasn't the deal."

"I know." I bow my head.

"Then you know what happens next," she says.

"I'm grounded?"

"Right, and we're going to talk about your choices and why they were wrong when we get home, but first," Mom sits, patting the chair beside her, "tell me what happened."

I go over the events, adding Tya at all the appropriate times, trying to keep the tears and my guilt at bay. Finally Mom brushes the hair out of my face and runs her thumb over my damp, salt-raw cheeks.

"I love you," she says, kissing my forehead, "and I'm sorry you had to go through this."

"If I hadn't played along, Rick wouldn't have done that to me," I sniffle.

Mom shakes her head. "No. This didn't happen because of anything you did or didn't do. It happened because Rick is a sick person and he made the decision to hurt you. You didn't do anything to deserve it and it's not your fault."

My stomach twists. It would be easier to believe her if I wasn't covering up so many lies. "I love you, Mom," I say, the tears coming again.

She wraps me in her arms as tight as when I was a small child waking up from a nightmare. Tight enough to ward off monsters. Moments later a policewoman clanks into the room, and I have to tell the story again.

★★★ CHAPTER TWENTY-ONE

DROP THE CHARGES

It's Sunday, the last day of Otafest. I should be showing off my costume, not sitting here running my fingers over the ripped fabric where my Ouran Academy patch used to be. I yearn for that patch. It was going to remind me of my first anime convention. Sadly, both it and any hope of a positive memory are gone.

The "talk" didn't happen last night. Mom and I were both too exhausted by the time we got in. Even so, Rick's words, his rough grip, and his snarling face kept chasing sleep away. At least they caught Rick, or rather, Paul and the twins did. They called the police once they found him, then gave their statements down at the station. Rick was arrested. I'm grounded. Mom's working. No one is having any fun today. And to top off all these good times, Mom and I are having the talk tonight.

I feel sick.

To keep from getting in any more trouble, I'm going to have to lie again. Again and again and again until I dig myself a hole beyond escape. Tya was with me. Tya wasn't at the dance. Tya was late.

Tya was in Jamaica.

Would it hurt so much to tell the truth? Is this what it means to be grown up? I'm such a fraud.

I try to ignore everything and read comics, but Batgirl's battles get mixed up with Rick's attack and I end up curled in a ball on the bed wishing Black Rock Shooter was real. She could take away this pain. Destroy the fear and anxiety with her big gun and make them disappear forever. But here in the real world, there are no superheroes and no one is going to save me.

I let out a long sigh as my phone chirps an incoming text. I pick up the phone and read it. It's Tobias saying, *Stop lying. Drop the charges.*

A cold wave hits me. Rick has obviously been talking to him.

The phone chirps again. *I mean it,* Tobias says.

I turn the phone to mute. Turn off the vibrate. Try to think of something else, but five minutes later I'm checking. Twenty-three messages, all telling me to drop the charges.

It goes on for pages.

Leave me alone, I type back.

I will, once you drop the charges.

He's lying, I respond.

You're lying, Tobias counters.

"Go away!" I scream, punching the letters.

Drop the charges. He returns. *Drop the charges. Drop the charges. Drop the charges.*

I throw the phone on my bed and pace the room. Then I pick up my phone and dial. "Hey!" Cora answers. "What's up?"

"Is Grandma Poitras around?" I ask.

"Um, yeah, just a sec."

I talk, and talk, and talk. I tell her everything. I tell her about Tya, Samir, Jemma, and Rick. I tell her about my feelings, and how guilty I am. How I wanted it to be real until it became too real. I tell her how I messed up and did everything wrong by running away from the people who could help me. I cry and I sniffle and I rant. Grandma Poitras listens to it all. Then she tells me I'm okay.

"I don't feel okay."

"You won't for a while," she says. "But you will be. Especially once you take your medicine."

"What medicine?" I ask.

"You know," Grandma Poitras says. "You absolutely know." Then she laughs. "It's not going to be easy, but things never are. Now talk to Rose."

We haven't spoken since Rose was raped. I still feel bad about that too. Like I should have known it was going to happen and done something to stop it.

"Uh, hi?" Rose's voice comes on the phone. "Mariam?"

"Yeah, hi. How are you?"

"Better," she says. "You?"

I pull my knees into my chest and lay my chin on them. "Not good. I had a close call. I can't stop thinking about it. I keep imagining how bad it could have gone and about what happened to you."

I hear Rose sigh on the other end. "I know. I did that too for a while. I kept thinking I could have died or worse. But I learned that you can't do that. You can't worry about what might have happened. You just have to focus on what did happen, and accept it. When you do that, things get better. Trust me."

"Are you better?"

"Not yet. Not all the way." She pauses. "Hey, my mom's here. I have to go." The phone clicks and the line is silent.

I take a breath. I think about everything Rick did. Not what he could have done, but what he actually did. I made it out with a few bruises. That's all. A few bruises and maybe some important lessons. I know I won't let this happen again.

Not ever again.

Another text comes in. Tobias again. *Drop the charges.*

My fear turns to anger. I'm not going be scared by a bully, or worse yet, a bully's sidekick. I'm not going to let anyone tell me what to do or compromise my feelings. I'm not going to be controlled.

Not anymore.

Grounded or not, this ends now.

I make a phone call to Samir then get to work packing what I need. Things like a whistle and the pepper spray Mom keeps hidden under her bed. Finally I text Tobias. *Meet me,* I tell him.

His reply is immediate. *Why?*

I want to talk.

Drop the charges and I'll meet you, he retorts.

Meet me and I might, I answer back.

There's a pause, then he answers. *Fine, where?*

★★★

Tobias is waiting in front of Another Dimension Comics when I arrive. Samir stands just inside. They both look angry. I feel the same.

"Why'd you do it?" Tobias yells before I even get to him.

I eye him. "Do what?"

"Lie."

"I didn't lie."

"Bullshit!" Tobias strides over to meet me, fists clenched, eyes wild.

I slip my hand into my satchel, fingering the pepper spray. "What did Rick tell you?"

"He said you tried to kiss him. That you were wanted to make it real. Then you freaked out and called the cops."

"That's the lie." I scowl.

"Prove it." Tobias smirks. "There was no one around,"

"I will," I say, "at the trial."

"Bitch!" Tobias spits.

"You know this isn't the first time Rick has pulled this crap."

"Nothing happened to that girl." Tobias crosses his arms over his chest. "Not like everyone said."

"Sure, maybe the rumours were exaggerated. But something happened. She wouldn't have quit the play otherwise. And we both know Rick was the one who did it."

Tobias charges forward, chest out, fist raised. He stops inches from my head. "Shut up!" he yells.

The comic shop door opens and Samir steps outside. "Mariam, need any help?"

I shake my head because, I don't. Not now that I know Tobias is all show. I loosen my grip on the pepper spray and pull my hand out of the satchel.

I walk around him asking, "Am I too close to the truth? The way he controls you should be enough to prove he has no respect for anyone but himself. So, how many will it take?"

Tobias squints at me, eyes following. "How many will what take?"

"How many girls have to get hurt before you'll believe that Rick has a problem?"

"He doesn't have a problem."

"So, more than two. Will five do the trick? Or ten? How about twenty? Or are you going to wait until he actually rapes one of his fantasy girlfriends before you stop standing by and do what's right?" I challenge.

"Screw you!" Tobias screams, his face going red to the tips of his ears. "He's not like that!"

"Not yet," I say, keeping my voice calm.

"You sure you don't need my help?" Samir asks, starting down the stairs.

I shake my head.

Sure, guys like Tobias and Rick, with their lies and manipulation, are intimidating. Scary even. But I can handle it. Me. Not Batgirl or Black Rock Shooter. Mariam. Because I have finally decided, I don't have time for people like that.

And that includes myself.

"Tell Rick," I say to Tobias, "two girls are enough for me. I'm the last one he hurts. I'm pressing charges. And if you keep harassing me, I'll press charges against you too."

Tobias clenches his teeth. "Why couldn't you just play along?"

"Because I don't need a fantasy to keep me happy. I like the real world."

Tobias's anger flows off of him like desperation. He turns and runs in the direction of the C-Train, flipping me the finger over his shoulder.

Samir chuckles. "You are one brave girl." He opens the door to the comic book shop, holding his arm wide. "Want to come in? We can talk Batgirl and stuff. It's pretty quiet right now."

I shake my head. "I've had enough of that for a while, but thanks — for last night and today."

"No problem." Samir smiles, briefly melting my heart with his beautiful brown eyes. "Come by when things settle down. Maybe we can hang out." He laughs. "You know my hours."

I nod and walk away, my pulse pounding. Going into the comic book shop with Samir is what I want to do, but I don't have that luxury. I have to do what is needed instead.

CHAPTER TWENTY-TWO

GIVE ME A CHANCE

"Mariam! What are you doing here?" Mom calls from the counter, coffee pot in hand.

Mei, her friend and boss, gives me a friendly scowl. "Aren't you supposed to be grounded?"

I nod. "Can we talk?" I ask Mom.

"Yes, yes," Mei says, snatching the coffee pot out of Mom's hand and shooing her towards an empty table. "Go, go, you've been miserable all day."

I sit at the table. Mom joins me. We look at each other and say nothing. Mei rushes two cups of coffee to us, smiles, and leaves to greet some new customers who come in the door.

I clear my throat. Bite my lip. Wish this was over already. "Mom," I finally say, "I need to tell you something. I lied and I feel really bad about it."

"I see," Mom says. "What did you lie about?"

Setting my eyes on my mom's, I jump in. I tell her everything, from Tya's trip to Jamaica, to the Black Rock Shooter costume, to Rick and his friends. I even tell her how seeing Samir and Jemma on the day she dropped me off was just a coincidence. I lay it all out, barely stopping for a breath. Finally

I say, "You've always taught me the truth is the most important thing in the world and I didn't honour that. I'm sorry."

Mom sips her coffee. I sit rigid. Waiting.

"I'm sorry too," Mom finally says. "I've always thought of you as honest. You've ruined that."

I grab Mom's hand. "I am going to be from now on. I've learned my lesson. I promise."

"So you say," Mom replies, "but what about the next time you want to do something you know I won't agree with? Are you going to ask or are you going to sneak?"

I think about that. Can I follow all of Mom's rules right until I'm eighteen? Even the ones like not going to things alone or not talking to boys without another girl there? What if I like someone? What if it's Samir? "If I had asked to go to Otafest alone, would you have said yes?" I ask.

Mom shakes her head.

"Would you have gone with me so I could go?" I push.

"Not in that outfit you wore!" Mom scowls.

"What about my other one? The schoolgirl one?"

"I don't know. Probably not," she admits. "It's not really my thing."

"But," I frown, "how does that help keep me honest?"

"*I* have to keep you honest?" Mom snaps. "No! I have to keep you safe." Her voice drops. "There's just us now. That's it. What would I do if I lost you?" She stares at the table. "It scared me to death when I got that call last night."

"I was scared too," I admit. "I never thought a guy who acted so nice could be so controlling."

"There are all kinds of men," Mom says. "Just because they aren't shouting or grabbing doesn't mean they're nice people."

"I know. I get that now," I say.

"Good. Then you understand why I don't like you being around them."

"Yeah, but there are nice guys too," I say, thoughts of Samir jumping into my head. "How will I ever be able to tell the good ones from the bad if I never get to be around any of them?" I spread my hands. "What about my freedom? What about my chance to grow?"

"I give you plenty of freedom." Mom glares.

"Do you?" I ask. "I can't go to events by myself, I can't hang around with boys, and I can't get a job besides babysitting. Mom, I'm almost seventeen. Let me live."

"You're not a real superhero you know. You could get hurt."

"I know and that's terrifying." I take a breath before continuing. "But the thing is, I can learn from that hurt. And I need to learn so I don't make even stupider mistakes."

"Hmph." Mom sips her coffee and looks out the window. "You don't know how bad it can get," she says.

"I have a clue," I reply, "but I don't want it to stop me from living and working."

"Working?" Mom raises her eyebrow.

"Yeah. I want something that pays more than babysitting so I can help with the rent and stuff. Like you said, there's only the two of us. Please, let me have a chance."

"What if something happens to you?"

"Things *are* going to happen to me and not all of them bad. But please," I take her hand in mine, "please, while you're still here to guide me, let me try."

Mom says nothing, her lips a tight, pale line.

I continue. "You say you don't want me pretending to be a superhero. Fine. Help me live in the real world. The whole thing, not just parts of it."

She covers my hand with hers, sandwiching it in a gentle squeeze. "Maybe I could," she says, "but no boys until you learn that you don't run from a room full of people to a place where you're alone. That was stupid."

I smile. "Yeah, I figured that out about halfway through."

"And no going to things by yourself unless you're checking in regularly."

"I can do that. What about work?"

Mom hesitates.

"I really want to help," I insist. "You shouldn't have to do it all by yourself."

Mom lets out a huff and calls to Mei. "Do we still have those dishes to do?"

Mei nods. "A big pile of them. The floor could use a cleaning too now that we lost that part-timer."

Mom gives me a good look over, and bobs her head. "Fine, you can help in the back. But only in the back. At least right now. And that's when you're aren't studying or babysitting."

"Do I get paid?" I ask.

Mom shakes her head. "Prove to me you are going to be trustworthy and when I'm satisfied, we'll discuss it with Mei."

"Is that my punishment?"

"Do you want more?" Mom asks, raising an eyebrow.

"No! No, that's fine." I say holding up my hands.

"And you're still grounded."

I laugh. "Yeah, I kind of figured." We stand up and hug. "Thanks, Mom."

"I still don't like you growing up," Mom whispers in my ear.

"Sometimes I don't like it either," I whisper back.

★★★ CHAPTER TWENTY-THREE

HERO

I wave to Samir as I pass the comic book shop. He waves back, a smile plastering his face. He knows I can't go in and see him. It's going to be a while before I'm out of the doghouse and back to having real freedom. Still, Mei is paying me now and I'm still babysitting for Mrs. Bin, so things are better.

I round the corner and walk the two blocks to the diner. The jerk who keeps harassing my Mom steps right in front of me. Hand on the door. My gut squeezes, anger rises.

I hate this guy.

"You!" I say, grabbing the back of his shirt to get his attention.

He spins around. "Hey," he grins. "It's the girl who thinks I'm sexy."

"Yeah, not so much," I sneer. Behind me on a bench is the lady who busks with her drum. I bring her a coffee every time I work. She has my back. Up the street are a couple of skateboarders. Across the road are two moms with strollers and a pack of businessmen. Inside, my mom. I think I have my bases covered — even if this is an incredibly stupid move. "Find another diner," I tell him.

His eyes narrow and he leans back, fingers clenching his newspaper. "What?"

"Find another diner. You're not welcome here," I repeat.

"Says who?"

"Says me."

He pokes his thick and stubby finger in my face, leaning in. "No little girl is going to tell me where I can and can't go."

"Want to bet?"

His fist tightens on his newspaper, pulling it back threateningly. "Sure."

I smile, but it's far from friendly. "There are at least seven witnesses on this street alone, one of whom is my friend. And, I'm a teenager. I can call 911 before you get anywhere near me. So," I nod at his raised hand, "take your chances."

His arm drops inch by inch. "I'm still going in," he says.

I motion to the door. "Go ahead."

He grabs the handle, looking confused, then turns towards door, pulling it open.

"But know this," I say, making him stop mid-movement, "the second your hand touches any woman in there, the minute you say something out of line, or even look at anyone the wrong way, I *will* be calling the cops."

He stops moving.

"Got it?" I ask.

He lets go of the door. It glides shut. "You're a bitch," he says.

"No," I smile. "I'm a hero. A regular, everyday hero."

The jerk strides away. I go inside, shaking a little with adrenaline. Mom smiles from the counter, none the wiser. I decide to keep it that way. At least until she asks.

"Your friend dropped in," Mom says, pointing to a table by the window.

Tya looks up from her manga and waves. I glance at my watch. I still have fifteen minutes before I'm supposed to start.

"Is it okay?" I ask.

Mom nods. "Sure. But make it quick."

I head over and pull up a chair. "You're back! How was Jamaica?" I ask.

"All right. I got to watch Uncle Otto get drunk and dance on the table with my Grandma at the wedding. Who could ask for more?"

"Did you get a video?" I laugh.

"Are you kidding? Blackmail is the main way I pay for all my cosplay supplies."

"You are evil."

Tya winks. "Guess what? My mom felt so guilty about making me go to Jamaica instead of Otafest that she got me a year's subscription to this awesome anime site. You have to come over after school one day and watch it with me."

"I can't," I say. "When I'm not working or babysitting, I'm grounded."

Tya's smile slips. "Oh, right. Sorry about that. It was kind of my fault."

I shrug. "Not really. I could have told my mom the truth right off the bat."

"Would she have let you go?"

"Not at first, but we could have talked about it." I heave a sigh. "It would have made things less awkward."

"It will get better. My mom and I end up in at least three huge fights a year. Things always work themselves out."

"This is my first time."

"Seriously? Wow! That's insane. What are you? The

best-behaved kid in the universe?" Tya starts giving me a thorough look over. "Are you a cyborg or something?"

I laugh. "Stop it! It's just that Mom and I are really close. Now things are weird."

"Yeah, well, you're not her little baby anymore. You're growing up and moving on. It's freaking her out. Or, at least, that's what my mom tells me," Tya says. "Do you think she'll let you go to Otafest Aurora?"

"What's that?"

"An anime festival in November." Tya grins. "I'm totally wearing my Black Rock Shooter costume to it. You did a great job, but I'm going to rock that outfit."

"I'll have to ask. No promises."

"If you can go, what will you cosplay?" Tya leans in, waiting.

"I might just go as myself," I say.

Tya laughs. "High school student by day. Mariam by night. It's Dishwashing Girl!"

I put up my hands. "Good enough for me. At least right now."

"Well, at least think about it. I'll be there this time and cosplay is more fun with friends."

"Maybe."

Tya takes a drink from her tea, before asking, "Did any of those guys from that Ouran club call you afterwards?"

I nod. "It's the funniest thing. First Hyun called asking if I was okay. Then Sung called right after asking the exact same thing."

"That's almost creepy," Tya says. "Are you going to meet up with them?"

"I'm still grounded," I say tapping Tya's head with my forefinger. "Besides, I don't know if I want to hang out with people who put up with someone like Rick."

"I hear you," Tya says. "I'm still sorry that happened. Some people are completely crazy. At least you ran into Samir again. Will you be seeing him?"

A grin creeps onto my lips, even though I'm trying to play it cool. "Well, he does work at the comic book store, so . . ."

"Hey, I forgot to tell you," Tya interrupts. "I just found out. Our school has a cosplay club."

"Really?"

"Yeah, Sierra from art class told me. She saw the photos I posted of the Black Rock Shooter costume. We should totally join," Tya says.

"Still grounded," I reply. "Besides I told you, I don't know if I want to do that anymore."

"Hey, the more friends we make, the more people we can go to cons with, and the safer you'll be. Besides, there are lots of fully covered characters out there. You could be a member of the Black Magic club. Their cloaks cover their whole body. Not even their face is showing. You can't get more prudish than that."

"I'll think about it," I say. "Maybe I'll join in September."

Tya looks at me, serious. "It's going to be okay, you know. I'm here for you. You're going to be fine."

"I know." I nod. "I just need some time."

Tya smiles big, her braces glinting. "Well if that's the case — spend your time watching *Free! - Iwatobi Swim Club*. It's amazing! Watch for the muscles, stay for the story. I have a gift subscription for forty-eight hours to the anime site I can give you. You can power watch the whole series in thirteen hours or so. It will be awesome!" Tya bounces in her chair.

I grin. I know it's her way of helping me. I appreciate it. And she's right. Mariam, average high school student, is going to be just fine.

Mom waves and points at the kitchen door. "Dishes are waiting," she calls. "Time for work."

Right after I get the dishes done.